Aberdeenshire
COUNCIL

Aberdeenshire Libraries
www.aberdeenshire.gov.uk/libraries
Renewals Hotline 01224 661511

'I almost didn't recognise you.'

Noelle froze. She didn't have to turn around to know who was speaking to her. She hadn't heard that low, rumbling growl of a voice in ten years.

Slowly she turned and faced her former husband. The first sight of him in the shadowy foyer jolted her to the core. His hair was cut close, almost a buzz-cut. A long, livid scar of puckered reddened flesh bisected his right cheek, starting at his hairline and snaking all the way down to his jaw.

'And I almost didn't recognise you,' she said, keeping her voice crisp even though her knees were near to buckling just at the sight of him.

He seemed taller and darker and *bigger* than before, although that was surely an illusion. She'd just forgotten the effect his presence had on her, the way he held himself so still and yet with such authority. The man she'd fallen in love with.

She gave him as level a look as she could. 'What do you want, Ammar?'

'You.'

Kate Hewitt discovered her first Mills & Boon® romance on a trip to England when she was thirteen, and she's continued to read them ever since. She wrote her first story at the age of five, simply because her older brother had written one and she thought she could do it too. That story was one sentence long—fortunately they've become a bit more detailed as she's grown older. She has written plays, short stories and magazine serials for many years, but writing romance remains her first love. Besides writing, she enjoys reading, travelling and learning to knit.

After marrying the man of her dreams—her older brother's childhood friend—she lived in England for six years, and now resides in Connecticut with her husband, her three young children, and the possibility of one day getting a dog.

Kate loves to hear from readers—you can contact her through her website: www.kate-hewitt.com

Recent titles by the same author:

THE DARKEST OF SECRETS
KHOLODOV'S LAST MISTRESS
MR AND MISCHIEF
  (The Powerful and the Pure)
BOUND TO THE GREEK

Did you know these are also available as eBooks?
Visit www.millsandboon.co.uk

THE HUSBAND
SHE NEVER KNEW

BY
KATE HEWITT

First published in Great Britain 2012
by Mills & Boon, an imprint of Harlequin (UK) Limited.
Harlequin (UK) Limited, Eton House, 18-24 Paradise Road,
Richmond, Surrey TW9 1SR

© Kate Hewitt 2012

ISBN: 978 0 263 22789 5

Harlequin (UK) policy is to use papers that are natural, renewable
and recyclable products and made from wood grown in sustainable
forests. The logging and manufacturing process conform to the
legal environmental regulations of the country of origin.

Printed and bound in Great Britain
by CPI Antony Rowe, Chippenham, Wiltshire

THE HUSBAND
SHE NEVER KNEW

CHAPTER ONE

AMMAR TANNOUS scanned the crowded ballroom of the Parisian hotel with a coldly dispassionate air, his mouth a compressed line. Somewhere amidst this glittering throng his wife waited. Although *waited*, he acknowledged, was the wrong word; Noelle had no idea he was here. She might not even know he was alive.

He narrowed his eyes as he shouldered his way through the crowd, noting the way conversations sputtered into silence, followed by the hiss of surprised speculation. The newspapers, he knew, had carried the story of his miraculous escape from a helicopter crash two months ago, although he hadn't been front page news. He never was. Ammar always kept a low profile; working for Tannous Enterprises required he maintain an intense privacy. Still, some here recognised him.

'Mr Tannous...' A thin, nervous man approached him, looking, Ammar saw, not just nervous but scared out of his wits. Ammar tried to place the face, but he had done business with too many people to recall every frightened underling who had experienced the punishing power of Tannous Enterprises's fist. 'I was going to make an appointment...' the man stammered, fluttering his hands in apology. 'Once I heard the news...'

The news that he was alive. Not very good news for

most people, Ammar knew. Now he remembered the man, if not his name. He had a small clothing factory outside Paris and Ammar's father had become lien-holder. He'd called in the loan just before his death in an attempt to bankrupt the man and cease his paltry competition with Tannous's own interests.

'I'm not here about that,' Ammar said tersely. 'If you wish to make an appointment, call my office.'

'Yes...of course...'

Without another word Ammar moved past him. He could have assured the man he wasn't going to enforce his father's claim, but the words stuck in his throat. In any case, he didn't want rumours to start flying, or his business associates and allies to wonder or worry.

All he wanted was Noelle.

It had been her face, the memory of her smile that had driven his survival. When he'd been starving and dying of thirst, wounded and feverish, he'd longed for her. He might not have seen her in a decade, he might have sent her away only months after they'd married, but he intended to find her now...and finally claim her as his wife.

His expression grimmer than ever before, Ammar moved forward through the crowd.

'Someone is looking for you, and he seems rather ferocious.'

Noelle Ducasse turned at the sound of her friend Amelie's voice, a smile firmly curving her lips, her flute of champagne held aloft. 'Oh, really? Should I start quivering?'

'Perhaps.' Amelie took a sip of her own drink as she surveyed the crowd. 'He's about six foot four with a near-shaven head and a horrible scar on his face. The whole look is rather sexy, mind you, but also a bit fearsome.' Amelie raised her elegantly plucked eyebrows, clearly curious. 'Does that description ring a bell?'

'Not really.' Noelle gave her friend, always prone to exaggeration, a bemused look. 'He sounds like an ex-convict.'

'Maybe. Although his tuxedo is top of the line.'

'Intriguing.' Although she wasn't particularly intrigued. Paris's social scene was always buzzing. 'My feet are killing me,' she said as she deposited her half-empty glass of champagne on a tray held by one of the many circulating waiters. 'I might call it a night.'

'I knew those heels would murder you.' Amelie spoke with gleeful satisfaction; she'd wanted to wear the five-inch silver stilettos that had been seen on the catwalk at Paris's Autumn/Winter Fashion Week last March. Arche, the high-end department store they both worked for as assistant buyers, would sell them exclusively this autumn.

Noelle shrugged philosophically. 'All part of the job.' Arche liked to have its junior buyers out and about in Paris's social scene, modelling Arche fashions and looking glamorous. After five years, Noelle was tired of playing at being a pretty young thing, but she knew it was all about paying her dues. In another few months she'd be up for a promotion to senior buyer of women's wear, instead of focusing just on shoes and accessories.

'You can't leave yet,' Amelie protested with a pout, 'it's only eleven.'

'And I have work tomorrow. As do you, I might add.'

'What about your ferocious admirer?'

'He'll just have to admire from afar.' A flicker of curiosity rippled through her—a shaven head and a scar? Really? In this crowd of preening socialites it seemed unlikely. Still, all she wanted now was her bed and a hot drink. And a good book. Her scary suitor would have to live with disappointment.

She waved her farewell to Amelie, who had already moved on to the next crowd of social-climbers. Standing alone amidst the circulating crowd, Noelle suddenly experienced a sharp pang of loneliness, the kind she'd tried not to let herself feel in the ten years since she'd walked out on her marriage and rebuilt her life—a life she'd chosen, even if it bore no resemblance to the kind of life she'd expected to have. She liked Amelie and all of her other friends, but they weren't kindred spirits. Soulmates. But then she'd given up on that idea long ago.

Sighing, she pushed any recriminations, as well as that irritating pang of loneliness, to the back of her mind. She just wanted to go home. In bed with a book and a hot drink she'd feel better. And at least she'd be able to shed these ridiculous shoes.

It took her a quarter of an hour to work her way through the crowd, knowing she needed to stop to smile or chat with various guests. She'd just reached the deserted foyer of the hotel when she heard a voice behind her.

'I almost didn't recognise you.'

Noelle froze. She didn't have to turn around to know who was speaking to her. She hadn't heard that low, rumbling growl of a voice in ten years. He still, she acknowledged distantly, spoke with the cautious reserve of a man who chose his words with care and didn't say many of them.

Slowly she turned around and faced her former husband. The first sight of him in the shadowy foyer jolted her to the core. His hair was cut close, almost a buzz-cut. A long, livid scar of puckered reddened flesh bisected his right cheek, starting in his hairline and snaking all the way down to his jaw. He was, she knew then, the ferocious admirer Amelie had told her about. Ammar. She should have considered such a thing, she supposed, although in truth she'd never have expected Ammar to be looking for her. He'd never looked for her before.

'And I almost didn't recognise you,' she said, keeping her voice crisp even though her knees were near to buckling just at the sight of him. He seemed taller and darker and *bigger* than before, although that was surely an illusion. She'd just forgotten the effect his presence had on her, the way he held himself so still and yet with such authority. The way his mouth thinned and his eyes narrowed—so different from the man she'd thought she knew. The man she'd fallen in love with. She gave him as level a look as she could. 'What do you want, Ammar?'

'You.'

Her heart thudded hard in reaction to that simple statement. She'd asked him once before what he'd wanted, if he wanted her. Then the answer had been a resounding and devastating no. Even now, ten years later, the memory made her burn with painful humiliation, the remnants of the utter heartbreak she'd felt at the time. 'How interesting,' she said coolly, 'considering we haven't even spoken in a decade.'

'I must talk with you, Noelle.'

She shook her head, hating how autocratic he sounded. *Still*. 'We have nothing to say to each other.'

He kept his gaze steady on hers, solemn and fierce. 'I have something to say to you.'

She felt a sudden, hot clutch of emotion in her chest, a burning behind her lids. *Ammar*. She'd loved him so much, so long ago. She hated that she felt even a remnant of it now. And whatever he wanted to say to her…well, she didn't want to hear it. She'd opened herself up to him once before. She would not do so again.

He stepped closer, and she saw how gaunt he looked.

He was powerfully built, every limb corded with muscle, yet clearly he'd lost a significant amount of weight.

'You heard about my accident,' he said, and she realised she'd been staring at him quite openly.

'Yes. My father told me. And about your miraculous rescue.'

'You don't sound particularly pleased that I survived.'

'On the contrary, Ammar, I was glad. No matter what happened between us, I've never wished you ill.' For too long she'd wanted him back. But she wasn't about to succumb to that ridiculous temptation now, not even for a moment. 'I'm sorry for your loss,' she said stiffly. 'Your father.' Ammar just shrugged.

Noelle stared at him, wondering just how he had come to this moment. She knew the bare facts: two months ago her father had rung to say Ammar had been killed in a helicopter crash, along with his father. He hadn't wanted her to find out through the media, and while Noelle had been grateful for that she hadn't even known how to react. Anger? Sorrow? It had been ten years since their marriage had been annulled, and even longer since she'd seen him, yet the pain of their failed relationship had hurt her for years.

Mostly she'd just felt numb, and then as the weeks had passed she'd probed the dark tangle of emotions underneath that comforting numbness and found the main feeling in that confusing welter was regret, a sense of loss for what she'd once believed they could have had together, the happiness that had been stolen away with such sudden cruelty.

Then a few weeks ago her father had rung again, told her Ammar was alive. He'd been rescued from a deserted island by a few men in a fishing boat and was returning to lead his father's business, Tannous Enterprises. The regret

Noelle was just coming to terms with suddenly solidified into the still-raw anger she'd been nursing all along. Damn Ammar. Damn him for breaking her heart, for rejecting her all those years ago and, most of all, for coming back now to stir up the painful emotions she thought she'd buried.

Now she pushed it all down and gave him a steely glare. 'Like I said, we have nothing to say to each other.' With her head held high she pushed past him.

Ammar reached for her arm. His fingers circled around her wrist, the heat of him seeming to sear her skin. Noelle stiffened, knowing he was too strong for her to attempt to pull away.

'Wait.'

'It appears I have no choice.'

Ammar let out a rush of breath. 'I just want to talk.'

'Then start speaking, because you have thirty seconds before I make a serious scene.' She glanced pointedly at the lean brown fingers still encircling her wrist. 'And I'd rather not have a bruise.'

Ammar dropped her wrist so suddenly her arm fell back against her side. She felt as if she should bear a mark from where he'd touched her, a painful red weal, but there was nothing. 'It will take more than thirty seconds,' he said tersely. 'And I have no intention of conducting a conversation in the foyer of a hotel.'

'And I have no intention of going anywhere with you.'

Ammar said nothing, just studied her, his head cocked, his narrowed amber gaze surveying her from top to toe. 'You're angry,' he finally said, an observation, and she let out a quick, humourless laugh. The last time she'd seen him she'd been crouching on the bed in his hotel room, holding back sobs, wearing only her underwear. He'd told her, very coldly, to leave. Yet even as that memory made her insides writhe, she quickly dismissed it. Ancient history.

She wasn't angry; at least, she shouldn't be. She definitely shouldn't still feel this hot rush of bitterness and hurt.

What she should have done tonight, she saw now, was acted coolly, politely indifferent. Maybe even reservedly friendly. She should have treated Ammar as an acquaintance, not the man who had broken her heart and crushed it under his heel. She never should have shown how much she still cared.

Because she didn't.

'I'm not angry,' she lied. 'But neither do I see any point in conversing with you.'

'You don't,' Ammar asked, the words seeming to scrape his throat, 'have any interest at all in what I might want to say?'

She stared at him, saw his mouth was twisted with bitterness, or maybe even sorrow. He looked different, and it wasn't just the scar or near-shaven head. It was something that emanated from his very self, from the hard set of his shoulders to the deep shadows under his amber eyes to the twisted curve of his mouth. He looked like a man who had endured far too much, who was near to breaking from it all.

For a breathless moment she felt that old savage twist of longing lying latent beneath the knee-jerk reaction of anger. She had the bizarre and yet achingly familiar urge to comfort him, to make him smile. To listen, and to understand—

No. Ammar Tannous had appealed to her curiosity and compassion before. She'd fallen in love with him, or what she thought she knew of him, and then he'd gone and hadn't just broken her heart but shattered her whole existence. It had taken years—*years*—to build up this new life, this new Noelle. She wasn't always sure if she liked what she'd made, who she'd become, but at least she owned it. She owned herself; she was strong, focused, needing no one. And a few minutes' conversation would never change that. She wouldn't let it.

'Go to hell, Ammar,' she said and walked past him, stumbling once in her ridiculous stilettos before she righted herself and stalked out into the night.

Ammar stared after Noelle's retreating back—so straight and rigid—and felt a pulse of fury beat in his blood. How could she walk away from him like that? She hadn't given him more than two minutes of her time, and all he'd wanted to do was talk—

And tell her, his mind mocked, *what, exactly?* He'd never been good with words, hated talking about emotions. Yet since the crash he'd known he needed Noelle back in his life. From the moment he'd regained consciousness, alone and injured on a tiny slice of deserted beach, he'd thought of her. He'd remembered her playful smile, the way she tilted her head to one side as she listened to him—not that he ever said much. As he'd battled fever he'd dreamed of her, the soft slide of her lips, her husky murmur of assent as she tangled her hands in his hair and pressed against him. He had even, incredibly, imagined sliding himself into her warmth and feeling her close around him, joyfully accepting the union of their bodies. That certainly belonged only in his delirium, for making love with Noelle was a pleasure he had never known.

And at this rate never would.

Ammar cursed aloud.

He'd handled their meeting badly, he saw that now. He shouldn't have cornered her, made demands. Yet what else could he have done? He was a man of action and authority. He didn't mince words. Most times he didn't even say please.

And Noelle had been his *wife.* Surely that should still

mean something to her; it did to him. Yet from the way she'd just stalked away, he suspected it didn't.

And yet…for a moment, a second, she'd looked at him the way he remembered. Her hazel eyes glinting with emotion, her face softening into a smile. He'd seen it, just for that one second, a flicker of happiness. He felt a faint, fragile hope at the thought. Yet how to talk to her? Make her listen?

Take what you want. Never ask. Asking is weakness. You only demand.

He heard his father's harsh voice echo through him, as if he was still alive, standing right next to him. Lessons he'd learned from childhood, words that were written on his heart.

He heard the screech of her taxi pull away and felt both tension and resolve steal through him. He'd told his brother Khalis that he wanted to find his wife and restore Tannous Enterprises. He wanted, finally, to build something good and right with both his life and his work. He would not let it end here, with Noelle stalking away from him. He would get her back. He would reclaim his business, his wife, his very soul. No matter what. No matter how.

As soon as she reached the pavement Noelle hailed a taxi. She slid into the dark leather interior and saw she was trembling. Her ankle throbbed from when she had stumbled. Irritated, she kicked off her stilettos and gave the driver her address on the Ile St-Louis.

Ammar. She couldn't believe she'd actually seen him. That he wanted to talk to her. *Why?* No, it was better this way. Better not to know, or even to wonder. She had nothing to say to him any more and that was all that mattered.

But once you had so much to say to him. Closing her eyes, Noelle leaned her head against the seat. She saw herself at thirteen years old, all coltish legs and gap-toothed smile, squirmingly conscious of the spot on her chin. He'd come with his father to her family's chateau outside Lyon to talk business with her own; a rangy, sullen seventeen-year-old, he'd studiously ignored her until Noelle had made it her personal mission to make him smile.

It had taken her twenty long minutes. She'd tried everything: telling jokes, poking fun, sticking her tongue out, even a bit of clumsy flirting. He'd remained stony-faced, unspeaking, staring out at the sluggish Rhône that flowed past the bottom of their landscaped gardens.

In a fit of girlish pique, Noelle had flounced away— and fallen flat on her face. When she'd scrambled to her hands and knees, her face scorched with mortification, she'd seen a large callused hand reaching down to hers. She'd taken it and his fingers had closed over hers, causing a tingle to travel right up her arm and through her body, a delicious, spreading heat she'd never, ever felt before. Then she'd looked up into Ammar's face and saw his lips curve into the barest of smiles, no more than a glimmer, gone when she'd blinked.

'Are you,' he asked, seeming to choose his words with the utmost care, 'all right?'

With effort Noelle had risen, yanking her hand from his to swipe at the bits of dirt and gravel on her knees. Embarrassment came rushing back and she felt like such a child. 'I'm fine,' she said stiffly, but Ammar reached down and brushed her knee with his fingers.

'You're bleeding.'

She'd scraped her knee, just a little bit, and a few drops of blood trickled down her shin. She brushed them away impatiently. 'I'm all right,' she said again, still embarrassed.

To her utter shock, Ammar said in his restrained, careful way, 'Tell me that joke again.'

'Which one?'

'Toc-toc.'

They'd been speaking French, the only language common to both of them, and now Noelle obediently repeated the joke. *'Toc-toc.'*

'Qui est là?' Ammar asked, his tone so very solemn.

'S.'

'S...qui?'

'S-cargot!' Noelle finished triumphantly, and Ammar frowned for a second, his brow wrinkling as if he had never heard a joke before, and then he smiled. Properly.

That smile transformed not just his face, but his whole self. His body lost its rigid tension, his eyes lightened to gold, and the flash of white teeth—all of it together made thirteen-year-old Noelle very aware that this was an older and exceedingly handsome boy.

She looked away, flushing yet again, revealed by her blushes. 'It's a pretty stupid joke,' she muttered.

'I like it. *S-cargot*. Very good.'

They lapsed into an awkward silence, and a few minutes later his father came out of the chateau. He called once to Ammar in Arabic and she watched, strangely deflated, as he nodded and headed towards him.

'I like it,' she called at the last moment. 'When you smile.'

He glanced back at her, their gazes locking in what felt to Noelle like sweet complicity, and in that moment she thought with a sudden blaze of certainty, *I am going to marry him when I am older. I am going to make him smile all the time.*

She didn't see or speak to him again for nearly ten years, when they'd crossed paths in London and started dating, a tender courtship, the memory of which still made Noelle ache inside.

Yet in the space of a single day—their wedding day—he'd become a cold, hard stranger. And ten years later she still didn't understand why. Now, as the lights of Paris sped by in a blur, she told herself it was better that she'd left the hotel before he could have said anything. Before he could hurt her again.

Yet the next morning, as sunlight washed her bedroom in pale gold, Noelle was caught by another memory: twenty-three years old, walking with Ammar in Regent's Park in London, the sunlight filtering through the leaves. She had been chattering on endlessly, as she always seemed to do, and she'd stopped, self-conscious, and ducking her head had said, 'I must be boring you completely.'

'Never,' Ammar said, and his tone was so sincere and heartfelt that Noelle had believed him utterly. He'd cupped her cheek with his palm and Noelle had closed her eyes, revelling in that simple little touch. Except nothing had been simple or little about it; they'd been dating for two weeks and she was in love with him, had been in love with him for years, and she thought he might love her, even though he'd never said. He'd never even kissed her. Yet when they were together the world fell away and all Noelle could think was how happy he made her and how she wanted to make him smile, then and always.

He'd smiled then, cautiously, touching her cheek. She'd been so besotted she'd actually closed her eyes, tilted her face upwards. She might as well have worn a neon sign saying *kiss me*. And he had. The barest brush of his lips against hers, and yet it had been electric. Noelle had leaned into him, her hands clenching on the lapels of his coat, and he'd rested his forehead briefly against hers, the gesture tender and yet possessing a bittersweet sorrow she still didn't understand. She swayed against him and he steadied her, setting her apart from him.

She should have known then. Should have seen that no male as potently masculine and deeply attractive as Ammar Tannous would stop with a kiss. Would date her and not sleep with her. Marry her and turn away on his own wedding night.

The simple truth—the only truth—was that he'd never really desired her, never mind loved her, and he'd regretted their relationship entirely. He simply hadn't possessed the consideration to tell her so before it was too late.

She rolled onto her side, tucking her knees up into her chest, hating that she was raking up all these painful memories now. She'd stopped recalling them years ago, although it had taken a great deal of determined effort. One Saturday about three years after her marriage had been annulled she'd gone out with her parents for lunch at a swanky restaurant overlooking the Seine and said firmly, 'I'm over him now. But let's not talk about him ever again.'

They'd obliged, clearly relieved to know she was finally moving on, even though they'd been angry and heartbroken on her behalf when the marriage had ended. In retribution, her father had severed all ties with Tannous Enterprises, and in rather childish pique Noelle had been glad. No one had ever mentioned Ammar Tannous to her again; none of her colleagues or friends even knew she'd once been married to him. It had been so long ago, and neither her family nor Ammar's had ever wanted that kind of publicity. Noelle certainly wasn't about to offer the information. It was as if the marriage had never happened. She could almost convince herself it hadn't, until now.

Until Ammar had died in the helicopter crash that had killed his father, and then came back to life. Resurrected not just himself but all the memories and feelings she'd thought she'd buried completely.

She hated feeling anything for him now, even if it was only anger. Yet in the pale morning light she also regretted the way she'd acted last night, like a child in a tantrum. He'd had a near-death experience, for goodness' sake, and had been very ill. And she'd loved him once, or thought she had. Couldn't she, in gracious and compassionate understanding, have listened to whatever he had to say? *That* would have surely shown him she didn't care any more. And who knew? Maybe he'd only wanted to apologise for what had happened all those years ago. An apology she wasn't sure she'd accept, but still. It might have been nice to hear it.

Sighing, Noelle rose from the bed. If Ammar approached her again, she decided, she'd listen to him. Briefly. Maybe a conversation could give her some proper closure to their whole sorry relationship, for she had to admit that she hadn't found it yet, despite many desperate attempts. She surely wouldn't be feeling so restless and edgy now if she had.

Half an hour later, dressed in a slim grey sheath dress and black patent leather heels, her hair twisted into a sleek chignon, Noelle hurried out of her apartment on the top floor of an eighteenth-century mansion towards the Métro. She was running late and she barely registered the narrow, near-empty street, the only person an older woman in an apron slowly sweeping the porch opposite.

Then she felt a hand clamp hard on her shoulder, something dark thrown over her head, smothering all sight and sound and, before she could even think to scream, she was bundled into a car and speeding away.

CHAPTER TWO

NOELLE stirred slowly to life, like a swimmer coming up to the surface of the sea. Consciousness glimmered, a twinkling, faraway thing. She reached for it, desperate now to seize it, and opened her eyes as if weights were attached to her lids. She lay in a bed and all around her was dark with shadows, and in the distance she heard the drone of an engine, could feel the thrum of it through her body. She was on a plane.

Panic shot through her as she struggled to make sense of what had happened, what little she could remember.

She had been walking to work and someone had grabbed her. Thrown a blanket or bag over her head and taken her in a car. She'd kicked out at her assailant and her fingernails had connected with someone's face, raking along a cheek. And then someone had said something—in a language she didn't understand—and she'd felt a jab in her arm and then…nothing.

Terror clutched at her chest, grabbed her by the throat. She'd been kidnapped. Abducted in broad daylight from one of Paris's best neighbourhoods. Impossible and yet—here she was. On a plane—going *where*? And what did her captors want? Ransom? Her family was certainly wealthy enough to consider such an awful possibility. Or was it something else—something worse? Vague images of the modern-day slave trade danced through her mind and she tasted bile. She'd kill herself first, if she had an opportunity.

'You're awake.'

Noelle let out a stifled scream. In the near-darkness she hadn't seen the figure sitting in a chair in the corner of the room. She still couldn't make out his features, but she could certainly recognise his gravelly voice. *Ammar.*

'You,' she said, and her voice came out in a scratchy, unused whisper. She coughed and Ammar came forward to take the glass of water from her bedside table and hand it to her. Noelle took it, her fingers trembling so much that Ammar kept his hand wrapped around the glass, his fingers overlapping hers, and helped her to drink. She was too tired and too thirsty to resist this small solicitude, yet finally, with an effort borne of desperate fury, she pushed the glass away, spilling droplets on the silk coverlet. 'You kidnapped me,' she managed, trying to make it a question, because surely he wouldn't have done such a thing. Yet here he was, and so was she.

In the shadowy room she could not make out his expression at all. 'I told you, I needed to talk to you.'

Noelle let out a hoarse bark of disbelieving laughter and leaned back against the pillows. 'And that makes it acceptable, does it?'

'You didn't give me many options.'

'You didn't give *me* many options.'

'Sometimes,' Ammar said, 'extreme measures are necessary.'

'You take extreme to an entirely new level.' She shook her head, tried to untangle her emotions. She was shocked, yes, and definitely angry, but was she afraid? No, she didn't think so. If she were honest, she felt a treacherous tingle of relief that it was him and not some unknown thug. Or even just that it was him. And yet...*kidnapped.*

'I'm sorry that extreme measures were necessary in this instance—'

'Sorry? You talk as if you had no choice but to kidnap me, Ammar. As if I made you do it.' She closed her eyes, a sudden sorrow added to the welter of feelings inside her. 'You're blaming me for what you did. This feels very familiar.'

'I never,' he said in a low voice, 'blamed you for anything.'

She supposed that was true. It had just felt like it was her fault. One minute she'd been married, nurturing dreams of happily-ever-afters, domesticity and children and a little house outside Paris, and the next her husband was barely speaking to her, never mind anything else, with no explanation at all.

'Turn a light on,' she said, because she wanted to see his face. Ammar opened a shade on one of the windows, letting in a sudden stream of hard, bright sunlight.

In the unforgiving brightness he looked, Noelle thought, terrible. He was unshaven, the scar snaking down his cheek livid, red and raw. Although he was dressed in a pressed grey polo shirt and black jeans, he seemed more haggard and gaunt than he had last night. Last night—could it really have only been last night that she'd seen him at the charity ball? She didn't even know how much time had passed.

'Are we on a plane?' she demanded hoarsely.

'My private jet.'

'Where are you taking me?'

'To my home.'

'Alhaja?' She'd hated the island his father had called home, a prison-like bunker set in gorgeous gardens on a private island in the Mediterranean. She'd spent two lonely months there before she'd finally fled.

'No. Alhaja was never my home.' His voice was hard, dark. Noelle saw one lean hand clench into a fist against his thigh before he slowly, deliberately flattened his palm out once more. 'We're going to my private villa in Northern Africa, on the edge of the Sahara Desert.'

'You have a villa in the *Sahara*?'

Ammar gazed back at her levelly. 'Yes.'

'And you're taking me there?'

'Yes.'

Obviously. Yet she still struggled to understand, to *believe*. What could he possibly want with her? She closed her eyes, too tired to ask. She heard the creak of the chair as Ammar rose, and then her exhausted body suddenly pulsed with life as she felt his hand, callused, cool, on her forehead.

'You should sleep some more.'

'I don't want to sleep—' But she did. Already she felt herself sliding back into the safety of unconsciousness. Dimly, as if from a great distance, she heard Ammar speak.

'We'll be there in a few hours. I'll stay here until you wake.'

Noelle was too tired to resist. And as she tumbled back into sleep a small, strange part of her felt reassured that he'd told her he would stay.

Ammar watched Noelle's face soften in sleep and felt regret pierce him with its double-edged sword. Ever since he'd arranged for her transport here he'd felt it, that sliver of doubt, jagged, sharp and painful. He should not have taken her like that. Kidnapped, that was the word she'd used. A crime.

He sat back in the chair, his hands resting on his knees

as he gazed at her sleeping form. He shouldn't have done it, he knew that, but what choice had he really had? He was not going to chase her around Paris, trailing after her like a kicked puppy, begging for a few seconds of her time. And here, just the two of them, he hoped—even if he was unwilling to say it aloud—that they might recapture something of what they'd had before.

Now you'll know never to trust a woman. Never to be weak.

Even in death his father mocked him. Ammar swallowed hard, his throat suddenly dry, his heart thudding. He hated his memories. Hated the response they instinctively dredged up in him, the fear, the loathing. The longing. He forced them away, made his mind blank. He'd always been good at that, had *had* to be good at it. Don't think about what you're doing. Don't think about who it hurts. Don't think. Taking a deep, slow breath, he leaned back in the chair and waited for Noelle to wake.

When Noelle woke again the sluggish exhaustion had gone, giving her a sense of relief, but also leaving her feeling both weakened and wary.

She sat up and saw Ammar was still sitting in the chair by her bed. He'd fallen into a half-doze, his face softened in sleep, dark lashes sweeping against his cheek, reminding her for a breathless second of the man he used to be. The man she'd thought he was. His eyes flickered open and he stared at her for a taut moment that seemed suspended and separate in its sudden, raw honesty. Ammar gazed at her, seeming almost vulnerable, hungry, and as for her? Noelle could feel the answer in herself. She'd loved this man once, no matter how he'd brought them to this place, and she felt its echo through her heart.

Ammar straightened, glancing at his watch, and the moment broke. 'We'll be in Marrakech in twenty minutes.'

'And then?'

'A helicopter to my villa. It takes a couple of hours.'

She shook her head slowly, banishing that echo, that remnant of longing. 'Ammar...why are you taking me there? What do you want from me?'

His mouth tightened and his gaze flicked away. 'We'll talk about that later. Right now you should freshen up. There's food in the main cabin.'

'Don't tell me what to do.'

He returned his gaze to her, level and considering. 'As you wish. I was only seeing to your comfort.'

'My *comfort*? If you'd been concerned with that, you wouldn't have kidnapped me in the first place!'

He expelled a low breath. 'I told you, it was necessary.'

'You had me *drugged*.'

'It was the safest way to transport you. I didn't want you to harm yourself.'

'How very thoughtful of you.'

'I try,' Ammar said with a ghost of a smile, and it took Noelle a stunned second to realise he was actually making a joke. *Toc-toc.*

'Try harder,' she answered back, meaning to snap, but it came out like some absurd attempt at witty banter. It was getting harder to hold onto her brittle edge, the safety of sarcasm. She could still remember how he'd looked in that unguarded moment, how she'd felt, even as fury raced through her.

Ammar gazed at her with the remnant of that smile, his eyes dark and sorrowful. 'I will,' he said softly, and Noelle felt something twist inside her, start to break. No, she could not start responding to this man. Remembering.

The only thing to remember was the hard fact that he'd

hurt her terribly in the past and kidnapped her today. What kind of people did he know, to arrange a kidnapping in broad daylight? What kind of man *was* he?

Before their marriage she'd thought he was gentle, tender, loving, if a little restrained. They'd dated for three months, a time so achingly sweet Noelle's eyes stung to remember it. She'd wanted to give him everything, her life, her soul and, more importantly, she'd thought he wanted it. Sometimes she'd caught him gazing at her in a kind of wonder, as if he couldn't believe she was really his.

Then they'd said their wedding vows and in a matter of hours he'd changed completely, turned into a brusque and distant stranger she didn't know or understand. A man who, it seemed, was perfectly capable of abducting his former wife and keeping her captive in his desert villa. The real Ammar.

It was the real Ammar she needed to remember now. Drawing herself up, she said firmly, as if talking to an unruly child, 'Well, now you've got me here you can say whatever it is you've wanted to say, and then you need to arrange my immediate return to Paris. I can get a flight from Marrakech.'

Something flashed in Ammar's amber eyes, although Noelle could not discern what it was. She'd once loved the colour of his eyes, the warm peat-brown of whisky. She'd seen emotion reflected there, emotion he had never spoken of or given into in any way and yet she'd believed. She'd *known*.

'No.'

Noelle's fingernails snagged on the coverlet as she clenched her fists. 'No?'

'I cannot arrange your return to Paris. Yet.'

'When, then?' He shrugged, which was no answer at all. 'Ammar, what do you *want* from me?' Another flicker in his eyes—could it be regret? 'This is a crime, you know,' she said in a low voice, hardly able to believe she was saying the words, and that they were *true*. 'You could be arrested for this.'

He glanced away. 'I've done too many things already I could be arrested for. One more won't matter.'

Shock iced straight through her, froze in her bones. She did not want to know what he was talking about, was overwhelmed by the terrible strangeness of a man she'd once thought she knew. *Loved.* 'My God,' she choked, 'who are you?'

Ammar turned back to her and she saw a fierce blaze of determination now turning his eyes to gold as he met her own bewildered gaze. 'I'm your husband.'

She stilled, the cover sliding from under her nerveless fingers. 'You haven't,' she said after a long charged moment, 'been my husband for ten years.' And he'd never truly been her husband, never in the way that mattered most.

'I know that.' He looked away again, everything about him—his voice, his expression—seeming to harden. 'We'll talk of this later. We're about to arrive, and I'm sure you'd like a moment to compose yourself.' He rose from the chair. 'There are clothes in the wardrobe. I'll meet you out in the main cabin when you are ready.' He spoke coolly, issuing these instructions with every expectation of being obeyed. It reminded Noelle of the man he'd been after their marriage, and she hated it. Hated remembering how different Ammar had seemed, how different she'd been with him, confused, needy and so unhappy, her dreams turning to dust, hopes to ash.

'I'll stay here.' It was a small act of independence, but in her current situation it was all she could manage.

Ammar shrugged, then nodded his assent. 'Very well.' And then he was gone.

Ammar paced the main cabin of the plane, feeling as trapped as Noelle surely was. Nothing was going the way he had hoped. He'd handled everything wrong, he saw now, from the moment he'd accosted her in the hotel, to the clumsy abduction of her from the street, to the conversation he'd just had. He was a man who had millions at his disposal, thousands of employees to do his bidding and even more people who regarded him with both awe and fear, yet one slip of a woman defeated him. All the words he wanted to say, all the things he felt, tangled up inside him so he couldn't get any of it out. He didn't even know the words. He missed her, he wanted her, he *needed* her, but how he did tell her that without issuing a command?

Never show weakness. Never beg or even ask.

The rules his father had drilled into him were impossible to break or ignore. He'd learned them the hard way, by his father's fist, starting on his eighth birthday when Balkri Tannous had taken him from the playroom and his brother's side and, in the sanctified solitude of his study, hit him hard across the face without warning.

It had begun then and there, his education, the forming of his very self. How did he shed it? How did he *change*?

'Mr Tannous?' Abdul, one of his staff, appeared in the doorway. 'We land in ten minutes.'

'Very good.' He glanced back at the door to the bedroom and, after a second's hesitation he rapped on it sharply. 'We're about to land, Noelle. It would be safer for you to sit in here, in a proper seat.'

The door was wrenched open and Noelle stood there, still wearing her crumpled grey dress. She'd washed her face and brushed her hair, but he still saw dark shadows under her eyes, the anger flaring in their hazel depths.

She didn't speak as she moved past him and sat down, buckling the lap belt. Ammar sat across from her. He tried to think of something to say, some words to bridge the gulf between them, but nothing came. Kidnapping her had been just about the worst way to go about this. Yet how to make amends?

'I'm sorry,' he said abruptly, and she turned to face him, surprise flaring in her eyes.

'Sorry for what?'

'For...abducting you.'

'And do you think I should accept your apology?' She let out a short, unfriendly laugh and rolled her eyes. 'No problem, Ammar. Mistakes happen.' She shook her head, seeming disgusted, and fury flared through him.

'You wouldn't listen.'

'And you wonder why.'

He shouldn't have started this conversation. It was too soon. Ammar turned to stare out at the sky, an endless stretch of blue. He felt his stomach dip as the plane moved lower and then, a few minutes later, with the pair of them still sitting in taut silence, the plane bumped to a landing.

They didn't speak as they moved from the plane to the waiting helicopter. As they came out on the tarmac Ammar saw Noelle scan the empty expanse and wondered if she'd actually make a run for it. If she did he knew he could catch her easily and in any case he had half a dozen staff waiting for his command. Besides, they were in Marrakech and a woman alone with no money, no passport and no phone wouldn't get very far. Danger lurked everywhere.

For the first time he realised just how vulnerable she must feel, and regret lashed him again. He reached for her elbow, meaning to steady her, but she jerked away from him.

'Don't touch me,' she snapped.

Ammar dropped his hand. Wordlessly he ushered Noelle towards the helicopter and then climbed in after her.

They took off into the sky once more, neither of them speaking. Sweat prickled along the back of his neck and between his shoulder blades. He hated travelling in helicopters since the crash, but his villa didn't have the space to land a jet and there were no roads.

In any case, he needed to conquer his fear. Grimly, he stared out of the window, even as his stomach churned and memories of the crash danced before his eyes. He remembered the way the world had tilted and the sea seemed to swoop up to meet him. How he'd stared into his father's grim face, a man he'd loved and hated in equal measure.

'Ammar.'

He didn't realise he'd been scrunching his eyes shut until he opened them and saw Noelle. He felt a jolt of panicked confusion, for her face—her smile—had been the last thing he'd seen before impact. No more than a memory, and now here she was in reality. By his force.

'Are you all right?' she asked quietly, and he nodded. Gulped.

'I'm fine.' And even though he knew he'd revealed a terrible weakness, he couldn't keep from being glad she'd asked.

They didn't speak again until the helicopter had landed.

The whole world felt as if it were holding its breath as Noelle stepped from the helicopter. The air was hot and dry and utterly still. Desert stretched in every direction, endless, undulating sand, occasionally strewn with boulders and rocks. She didn't think she'd ever been in a more remote place.

Silently she followed Ammar into a low, rambling building of sandstone that blended almost entirely into its desert surroundings.

He stopped in the foyer, turned to her with that blank expression she despised. For a moment, in the helicopter, she'd felt a flicker of sympathy for him, knowing he must hate flying in helicopters since his crash. Sitting there so tautly with his eyes clenched shut, Ammar had looked like a man in the throes of a desperate agony.

And now? He looked as stony and remote as the desert surrounding them, and yet still, irritatingly, she felt that flicker. A yearning compassion she couldn't keep herself from feeling, even though she desperately didn't want to.

'Are you hungry?' he asked and, even though she knew she should resist any solicitude, Noelle nodded.

'Starving.'

'If you'd like to refresh yourself, there is a bedroom for you upstairs. And clothes, if you wish.' He glanced at her creased dress. 'You cannot wear that for ever.'

'It depends on how long you intend to keep me here,' Noelle answered bluntly and his expression tightened, eyes narrowing, lips thinning.

'We can discuss that at dinner.'

'Fine.' Noelle lifted her chin. She was strong enough to accept his hospitality—*ha*—and still keep swinging. With a jerky nod, she turned on her heel and headed upstairs.

She found a sumptuous bedroom behind the first door she opened, with a wardrobe full of clothes and an en suite bathroom with a sunken marble tub and an array of luxurious toiletries. After the day she'd had, she was ready for a good long soak.

Yet once she'd immersed herself in steaming, fragrant

bubbles, Noelle felt her resolve—and her anger—start to slip away. She kept seeing that look of yearning on Ammar's face when he'd woken up, when she'd caught him off guard. She felt the same yearning in herself, a longing for the way he'd been. The way she'd been, with him, so long ago.

That was not going to happen.

She couldn't start thinking that way, wanting that way. Not after he'd hurt her, not after he'd revealed what kind of man he was—

Do you really know what kind of man he is?

Refusing to answer that question, or even think it, Noelle dunked her head under the water and started to scrub. Too bad she couldn't scrub away her thoughts. Or that flicker of yearning that threatened to fan into something far more dangerous.

Ammar paced the dining room just as he'd paced the cabin of the plane. He came to his desert retreat for solitude and safety, a place where the rest of his life never intruded, yet he was finding neither tonight.

Should he let her go? The thought had been flitting around in his mind like an insistent insect since Noelle had suggested the very thing. If he let her go, Ammar knew, she would never come back to him. She would never love him again.

And the same thing might happen if you make her stay.

He closed his eyes. He'd felt hopelessness before, God only knew; he'd felt hopelessness for most of his life. Yet it hurt so much more when you felt hope first.

'Hello.'

He whirled around to see Noelle standing in the doorway.

'Come in.' He cleared his throat, took a step forward. He

felt tension twang through his body so he felt like a marionette, all awkward, jerky movements. He no longer knew how to be natural with her, but then had he ever? Being natural, he thought with a sudden bitterness, was not natural to a man like him. Yet there had been moments, miraculous, tender moments, where he'd felt himself lighten with the sheer joy of being in her presence. Smiling, even laughing, at her enthusiasm for life, her silly jokes, her sudden laughter. He missed that. He missed the man he'd felt he could be with her by his side.

She walked into the room and he saw she was wearing a caftan he'd ordered for her, along with all the other clothes. It was a pale spring green shot through with silver threads and, though it was basically a shapeless garment, it still somehow managed to emphasise her slender form, her graceful posture. Her hair was still damp from the shower and twisted up in a careless knot, her face flushed from heat—or anger. At that moment it didn't matter. All Ammar knew was that she was the most beautiful woman he'd ever seen.

'I'm glad—' he began, wanting somehow to articulate how lovely she looked, but she cut him off, her voice flat.

'I want my clothes back.'

He'd had his housekeeper take them while she was in the bath. He realised now how that might have made her feel even more vulnerable, and cursed himself for not thinking of that before. 'They're being laundered. You can have them back as soon as they're dry.' He'd regarded her stark grey dress and black tights with a sorrowful bemusement; the woman he remembered from ten years ago had worn bright clothes, cheerful colours. 'There is a wide selection of clothes at your disposal, in your room.' In addition to the caftan, he'd bought sweaters, shirts, jeans,

even a few dresses, all in the bright colours he liked—
and thought she did.

Noelle shrugged, the thin cotton of the caftan sliding
off one shoulder. Ammar's gaze was drawn instinctively
to the movement and he felt his insides tighten with long-
suppressed desire. Desire he'd never acted on, yet longed
to—had always longed to, even now. Her skin was the
colour of almonds, creamy and golden with a slight spat-
tering of freckles. 'None of them fit,' she said. 'They're
two sizes too big.'

'I thought I remembered your size.' He saw a flicker of
surprise in her eyes, like sunlight on water, that he would
have ever known such a thing.

'I've dropped a few sizes.'

'You've lost weight—'

'I'm thinner,' she corrected, and he frowned, because
Noelle had always been slender. Now that he was looking
at her properly, he saw how skinny she looked, the bony
angles of her elbows and collarbone jutting out even under
the voluminous folds of her clothing.

'Come eat,' he said and, with her mouth pressed into
a hard line, she followed him to the table laid intimately
for two.

This wasn't, Ammar acknowledged, going to be easy.
Yet he didn't want to let her go. He couldn't. Hope, he
knew, was too heady a possibility. Yet what would it take
to unbend her? Make her not just listen, but *want* to listen?

Grimly, he realised he had no idea.

Noelle stepped further into the room, deep with shadows
and flickering with candlelight, suppressing the sudden hot
flare of awareness she felt at the sight of Ammar's admir-
ing glance, quickly veiled. If he hadn't wanted her when

she'd been wearing a silk teddy and stilettos, he could hardly want her now, in this tent-like caftan.

In any case, it didn't matter what he did or didn't want. She was only here because she was hungry. And she needed to convince Ammar to return her to Paris.

'Please sit.' He pulled out a chair and, deciding there was no point in being ungracious, Noelle accepted and sat down. Ammar laid a napkin in her lap, his fingers barely brushing her thighs, yet even so she felt another flare of desire low in her belly. Never mind what he felt, she still had the same instinctive response to him. Lust and longing. *Hopeless.* How could she feel it now, after ten years, when he'd brought her here by force?

Resolutely, she pushed such thoughts away. Absolutely no point in dwelling on anything but a determination to get out of here.

'May I serve you?' he asked, so scrupulously polite, and it reminded Noelle of when they'd been dating in London. They'd got caught in a downpour and she'd brought him back to her flat in Mayfair, hoping he'd stay the night. She'd had a shower while he waited; she'd been far too shy to ask him to join her.

When she'd emerged, swathed in a dressing gown, her hair still damp, he'd asked, in that same serious, polite way, *May I brush your hair?* She'd nodded, and he'd so carefully, so gently, brushed her hair with long, sensual strokes. She'd had to keep herself from trembling throughout the whole exquisite ordeal, longing to lean back against him, for him to turn her around and take her in his arms. They'd kissed twice so far, that was all. Sweet, aching kisses that had made her want so much more. And for a moment she thought it would finally happen. Her hair finished, he'd laid the brush aside and his hands had slid slowly, deliberately along her shoulders, down her arms,

as if he were learning her body. Noelle had remained completely still, mesmerised by his touch, but she could not
keep from gasping aloud when Ammar pressed a tender,
lingering kiss to the bared nape of her neck. She'd never
experienced anything so romantic, so erotic, and so very
sweet. They'd remained there for an endless, aching moment, his head bowed, his lips against her skin, and then
he'd let out a shudder and stood up. Before Noelle could
even say anything he was, in his solemn, restrained way,
bidding her goodnight.

Now she glanced up at him, waiting patiently for her
response while she lost herself in all these aching memories. She was tired of them, exhausted by the emotions
they made her feel. Regret. Sorrow. Longing.

'Yes, thank you.'

He ladled couscous and stewed lamb on her plate, and
Noelle glanced around the room, spare and spacious, with
an understated elegance in its few pieces of mahogany fur-
niture. A pair of French windows were shuttered against
the night, and she wondered where they led. She'd opened
the shutter on her bedroom window after her shower, but
the only thing the moon had illuminated was the endless,
undulating desert and a long drop down to the sand.

For a short while she said nothing while she ate hungrily. 'So,' she said finally, stabbing another piece of meat
with her fork, 'why won't you return me to Paris?'

Ammar didn't answer for a moment. In the candlelight
he looked so serious, his eyes dark, his movements con-
trolled and restrained as always. Noelle glanced at the scar
snaking down his cheek. Amelie had been right; it did look
sexy. *He* looked sexy, but then he'd always been sexy to
her, sexy and gorgeous and infinitely desirable. Even now,
when he had lost weight—like she had—and still bore
the scars of his accident, she could not deny the pulse of

longing she felt for him. Her body remembered how he felt, the solid strength of him, corded muscle and callused skin. Even now, with all that had—and hadn't—happened between them, her body remembered and wanted more.

'I would like,' Ammar said, thankfully breaking into the torment of her thoughts, 'for you to stay here for a little while.'

Noelle jerked her gaze from its revealingly leisurely perusal of his body back up to his face with its implacable expression. '*Stay* here? For what, a little holiday?' Her voice was sharp with sarcasm but Ammar simply nodded.

'Something like that.'

'Ammar, you *abducted* me—'

He clenched one hand on the table. 'So you keep reminding me.'

'You think I can just forget it? I told you I had nothing to say to you, and I still don't. I want to go home.' To her shame, her voice trembled and she felt tears crowd under her lids. She wasn't even sure why she was near to crying: because she wanted to go home or because a tiny, treacherous part of her wanted to stay? How shaming. How pathetic. She bit her lip and looked away, not wanting him to see how close to tears she was, but she could not keep a shudder from ripping through her.

'Noelle—' His voice caught on a note of near-anguish and he reached one hand out to her, as if he would comfort her. How ridiculous was that, to be comforted by her captor? And yet she still longed for him to touch her, could almost imagine the warmth of his hand on her skin. She averted her head and he dropped his hand.

'Please, Ammar.'

'I cannot.'

'You can,' she insisted, angry now. Anger felt stronger, simpler. 'You brought me here; you can let me go. You just don't want to, and I have absolutely no idea why.' She glared at him, and Ammar gazed steadily back.

'I brought you here because I want to be with you,' he said, choosing each word with care.

Noelle blinked. Stared. Her mind seemed to have slowed down, snagged on his meaning. He wanted to *be* with her? 'What—'

'I want us,' Ammar said, 'to be husband and wife.'

CHAPTER THREE

As soon as he said the words, Ammar felt they were wrong. It was too soon; he shouldn't have revealed so much. He should have waited until she had relaxed a little, trusted him more. Yet how? *How?* He didn't know what to do other than issue orders, bark commands. And demand obedience.

Now her eyes widened and her mouth dropped open and she stared at him in what could only be described as horror.

'That,' she finally managed in a choked gasp, 'is impossible.'

Ammar felt the old instinct kick in. Defend. Deny. Don't ever admit any weakness. And hadn't he just done that, telling her he wanted to be married? *Husband and wife?*

Pathetic, romantic notions she obviously scorned. He sat back in his chair, his body rigid, everything in him fighting the awful sense of exposure he felt. 'Not,' he said coldly, 'impossible.'

'Impossible for me,' Noelle retorted. She looked angry now, angrier even than when she'd realised he'd had her kidnapped or told her he wouldn't take her back to Paris. Her cheeks were flushed and underneath the caftan her breasts rose and fell in ragged breaths. 'I have absolutely no desire to be married to you again, Ammar. To be *hus-*

band and wife.' He heard the contempt she put into the words and fury fired through him.

'This isn't about what you desire.'

She laughed, the sound hard and sharp. 'Obviously not, since you drugged and dragged me here—for God's sake!' She rose, throwing her napkin down on the table. 'This is the most absurd conversation I've ever had. Did you actually think, for a single second, that I would consent to being married to you again when you had to bring me here by force? When you completely and utterly rejected me in the worst way possible just months after we were married? Why on earth would I *ever* want a repeat of that heartbreak?' Her eyes flashed and her body trembled. Thunder and lightning. A storm right here, between them.

Ammar stared at her, his body pulsing with an anger he could not suppress even as he bleakly acknowledged she was right. He could not deny a single thing she'd said. 'We said vows,' he said tautly.

'Vows you broke the same day we spoke them! Where was the love in leaving me alone, waiting for you on our wedding night? Or how did cherish come into bringing me to that wretched island of your father's and leaving me there for *two months*?' Her voice broke and he thought she blinked back tears; her eyes were luminous with them. 'You hurt me, Ammar,' she whispered. 'You hurt me terribly.'

Ammar didn't answer. He couldn't; he had no words. He never had the right words, yet he hated that he had hurt her. The thought that he'd caused her so much pain—enough that it still made her cry years later—was unbearable; he forced it away, along with all the other thoughts that he couldn't face. There were, he knew, far too many of them. 'Then let me make it right,' he said. The words felt unfamiliar, awkward, and yet he meant them.

'How?' She swiped at her eyes, angry again.

'By giving our marriage a second chance.'

She stared at him, her eyes wide, like a trapped animal's. Then she looked away. 'Our marriage,' she said flatly, 'never was. Annulled, Ammar. Like it—we—didn't exist.'

'We did exist.' Sometimes he felt as if his time with Noelle, his *self* with Noelle, was more real than anything before or after. Yet he was not about to admit such a thing to her now.

She shook her head, her anger replaced by a weary bewilderment. 'Why do you even want such a thing? You didn't want to be married to me before. Why now?'

'I always,' Ammar said, 'wanted to be married to you.'

Her mouth dropped open and she looked as if she wanted to argue. Again. He looked away, fought the rush of painful fury he felt at revealing such weakness.

'I cannot believe that,' Noelle said flatly. 'I won't.'

'Why not?'

'Because—' She pressed a trembling fist to her mouth, her eyes still so heartbreakingly wide. 'Because it doesn't make sense.'

He knew it didn't. He felt the weight of all the things he hadn't told her, things he was afraid to tell her because he knew she would look at him differently. She would hate him, perhaps far more than she thought she did now.

'None of this makes any sense,' she whispered.

Ammar stared down at the table, took a deep breath. 'You loved me once.'

Silence. He looked up and saw her staring at him with such confused sorrow that it made everything inside him burn and writhe. Why had he said such a thing?

'Yes, I did,' she finally said. 'Once. But you destroyed that, Ammar, when you rejected me without any explana-

tion. You refused to come to me on our wedding night—
or any night after. Do you remember?'

He clenched his jaw so hard his whole head hurt. 'I remember.'

'You ignored me day after day, left me to rot on that
wretched island without so much as a word of explanation.
And then,' she finished, her voice breaking, 'when I came
to you and tried to seduce my own *husband*, you sent me
away in no uncertain terms!'

Every word she spoke was true, and yet still they made
him furious. He rose from the table, laying his palms flat
on its surface as he faced her and her accusing glare.
'Clearly there is no point in continuing this conversation.
You may return to your room and we will talk again tomorrow.'

She let out a harsh sound, something caught between a
sob and another sharp laugh. 'What is this, Ammar, *The
Arabian Nights*? Am I to be fetched day after day into your
presence until I finally break down and agree to your ridiculous demands?'

His head throbbed and he forced himself to speak
calmly. 'If I remember correctly, Scheherazade gained
her own happiness at the end of that tale.'

'And was threatened with death every day!'

'I am not threatening you,' Ammar said, suddenly unbearably weary. He did not want to fight her. He had not
wanted this bitter acrimony at all, and yet he recognised
it was at least in part his own damnable doing. 'You are
safe here with me, I promise you. But you are too tired and
it is too late for you to go anywhere tonight. Rest. Sleep.
We will talk tomorrow.'

'And then you'll let me go?'

He stared at her, saw the hungry longing in her eyes,
and felt a deep sorrow sweep through him. Once she'd

looked at him like that, with such desire and even love that it had both humbled and amazed him. And he'd driven her away from him on purpose. At the time it had felt like his only recourse; perhaps it was once again. Perhaps he sought the impossible. To change. To be loved once more, and truly. 'We'll talk tomorrow,' he said again, and to his shame his voice choked a little. He turned away from her and after a long tense moment he heard the gentle patter of her feet, and then the creak and click of the door opening and shutting.

He was alone.

Noelle slept terribly. Anger kept her awake at first, pacing the confines of her elegant bedroom. Ammar's house was deathly still, the only sound the whisper of wind on sand outside. She felt as if she'd landed on the moon.

And surely the evening's events belonged on a different planet—she still could not credit that Ammar wanted to restore their marriage. *I want us to be husband and wife.*

Why did that single statement send an icy thrill of terror and even excitement through her? Or was it simply shock? They'd never been husband and wife, not truly.

Even now Noelle remembered the ache of confusion and misery she'd felt, waiting for Ammar to come to her on their wedding night. They'd married at her family's chateau and planned to spend their wedding night in a private wing all to themselves. She'd gone to the bedroom, changed into a lacy and virginal peignoir she'd bought at a very exclusive boutique in Paris and, trembling with anticipation, had waited. And waited. And waited some more.

Once the doorknob had turned and Noelle had jolted upright from where she'd lain on the bed, desperate for him to come to her, only to hear someone's—surely Ammar's—

quiet footsteps pad back down the hall. The rest of the night had been spent in a lonely misery of confusion.

The next day they'd travelled to his father's home and base, Alhaja Island. Ammar had been horribly remote, barely speaking to her. Hesitantly, Noelle had asked him what had happened and he had said something about a business call, which had made her feel small and unimportant. A business call was more important than his own wedding night?

There had been no time for a proper conversation, and she'd been too young, too inexperienced and confused for a confrontation. She'd kept waiting for Ammar to change back into the man she knew and loved, but he never did.

That evening he'd flown to Lisbon for yet another business engagement. She'd remained on Alhaja, waiting for his return. Before their marriage they'd talked about setting up a house outside Paris, near enough the city for work but a good place for children, for family. She'd had it all planned out, the bookshop she would open in the Latin Quarter, the house they would buy, a cottage really, with wrought iron rails and a blue-painted door. She'd pictured it all, her work, her home, her life, all with Ammar. Dreams, she thought now, the old bitterness corroding her soul. Stupid, foolish dreams. She'd waited for two long, lonely months on Alhaja before she realised Ammar had no plans to return. And in a desperate last-ditch attempt to win her husband back, she'd flown to Rome to meet him.

It hadn't been easy; she'd had to call her father, coax him into letting her use his private jet. Balkri Tannous did not keep any means of transport on Alhaja, and so she'd been a virtual prisoner with the household staff, a silent, sullen crew. Her father had agreed, surprised yet able to deny her nothing—which Noelle had known—and through several begging phone calls to Ammar's staff, as well as a helpless-female act with the concierge, she'd contrived to find the name of his hotel and wait in his room dressed only in a silk teddy and stiletto heels.

What had happened afterwards Noelle could not even bear to think about.

Yet now, as she paced her bedroom, she felt her anger desert her and leave a welter of confused regrets in its wake. Why did Ammar want to resurrect their marriage? She had assumed all these years he'd completely forgotten about her but, no matter what either of them felt now, she could not pretend that was true. He hadn't forgotten. And neither had she.

Noelle sank onto her bed, exhausted by her own emotional wrangling. Anger was so much easier to deal with than doubt, yet she could not even cling to it.

You loved me once.

She had. At least, she thought she had, but had she really even known him? How could the tender, gentle man she'd loved have turned into a cold, unfeeling brute as soon as their vows were said? And what of the man he was now, and surely always had been?

I've done too many things already I could be arrested for. One more won't matter.

Noelle didn't want to think what he had meant by that. She'd learned, since the annulment, that Tannous Enterprises was said to be corrupt. She had harboured vague ideas of white-collar crime, had wondered if Ammar had been involved. She'd assumed, in an effort to gain some much-needed distance, that it was just more proof she'd never really known him. More evidence that any consideration or tenderness he'd shown her in those first few weeks had been nothing but a charade.

Now she wondered. Today she'd seen in Ammar a glimmer of the man she'd once loved, and it terrified her. What if that man—the tender man she'd once loved—was the real Ammar?

It would be so much simpler if she hated him. If he made her hate him. And surely she had enough reason to…and yet. And yet.

She didn't.

Eventually she fell into bed and a restless, troubled sleep. When dawn broke she felt no more refreshed, and had no more answers.

She showered and dressed, this time in a pair of jeans and a pale pink sweater she'd found in the wardrobe. They were too big, but not so much that she couldn't wear them. She cinched the jeans with a wide leather belt and rolled the sleeves up on the sweater. Had Ammar himself bought the clothes for her? It felt strangely intimate to imagine him picking things out for her, knowing her size. Her old size, at least, before she'd surrendered to Arche's ideal of feminine beauty, which was stick-thin and relentlessly plucked and manicured.

She opened the shutters on her bedroom window and blinked in the glare of the morning sun. The sky was a hard, bright blue, the desert a stark and endless stretch of sand. She could see nothing but sand and rock and sky. She swallowed hard and closed the shutters again.

I want us to be husband and wife.

His voice had invaded her dreams, and all night as she'd tossed and turned she'd endured a procession of memories she'd been trying to banish for years. Those poignant, tender days in London, when Ammar had seemed like a different man. The man she'd fallen in love with.

Well, he wasn't that man now. And, more importantly, she wasn't that woman, that naive girl who believed in love and wanted marriage and babies and a house in the country. She was a different person, stronger, harder and definitely more independent. She'd spent the last ten years building her career and making sure she needed no one. She sure as hell didn't need Ammar, and some time towards dawn she'd realised the best way to convince him to let her go was to show him just how different she was.

Resolutely Noelle headed downstairs in search of Ammar. She wandered through the marble foyer and several sparely elegant reception rooms before she found him in the back, in the kitchen. He stood by a floor-to-ceiling window that framed a sweep of sand, dressed in a worn grey T-shirt and faded jeans. His feet were bare and he held a mug of coffee as he stared out at the desert, a faint frown wrinkling his forehead, his eyes narrowed against the glare of the sun. For a stunned second everything in Noelle contracted with longing and regret. This was what she had wanted so desperately. A normal life, a normal marriage. Mornings with sunshine and the scent of fresh coffee and a hello kiss.

Well, she had two of those things today. Definitely not the third. She cleared her throat. 'Good morning.'

Ammar turned, his expression lightening a little as he took in her outfit. 'Not so bad,' he said, gesturing to her clothes. 'The fit.'

Noelle nodded tersely. She did not know how to act. Fighting every statement exhausted her, but being civil felt like a surrender.

'Coffee?' Ammar asked, and she nodded again. It seemed easier not to speak at all. She watched him move to the kitchen counter and pour coffee from the chrome pot. 'Do you still take cream and two sugars?'

'No,' Noelle said, and her voice sounded harsher than she intended. 'I drink it black.'

He arched one eyebrow in silent question and handed her her undoctored coffee. Noelle cupped her hands around its warmth, wondering how to begin. Ammar seemed different this morning, not approachable exactly, but less autocratic. She saw his laptop was open on the table, to a world news website. The moment felt, bizarrely and unbearably, normal.

'When did you stop taking cream and sugar?'

'About five years ago, when I started working for Arche.'

'Arche?'

'The department store I work for, as a buyer.' She glanced pointedly at the diamond-encrusted watch on her wrist, given to her by her father on her twenty-first birthday. 'I'm twenty-three minutes late for work right now, with no explanation. You might cost me my job, Ammar.'

He frowned. 'Working for a store, buying things? You used to work with books.'

'I changed careers.' Changed lives. The days spent in a dusty bookshop losing herself in someone else's happily-ever-after were over.

'When?'

'Ten years ago,' she said shortly, even though that wasn't quite true. It had been more like eight, but all those old dreams had died a quick death the night Ammar had pushed her away.

She'd turned away from them deliberately: a home, a family. A little house outside Paris and a bookshop of her own. She'd told him all about it, how the shop would have a little café, and toys for children, and original art for sale on the walls. 'A bit of everything,' he'd said, smiling, and her heart had felt so full.

Now she clamped down on all those memories and fixed him with a narrowed gaze. 'You don't know me any more, Ammar. I'm different and—'

'So am I.'

The breath rushed out of her lungs as she stared at him. 'What?'

'Different,' he repeated. 'At least, I am trying to be.'

She saw the corner of his mouth quirk upwards in a wry, self-deprecating smile and she felt that savage twist of longing inside her, making her remember when she didn't want to. 'I don't understand,' she said flatly, even though her heart was insisting she did.

'No?' He took a sip of coffee and half-turned away from her. 'Maybe it is impossible, anyway.'

In profile, Noelle could not keep from noticing—and staring at—the hard line of his jaw, the faint shadow of stubble on his cheek, the subtle pout of his lips. All of it together made her breath shorten and an overwhelming longing clutched at her chest. Lust and love. She'd once wanted him in every way a woman wanted a man. Protector, lover, friend. And now? She still wanted him. Her body yearned for him, her heart remembered. *No.* She set her mug down on the table. 'You really do need to let me go.'

He turned back to her. 'Do you like working for this Arche?'

'Like it? Yes. Of course. I mean—it's my job. My career.'

'And you enjoy this career?'

'Why do you want to know?'

His mouth quirked upwards again, ever so slightly. Almost a smile, and she felt another wave of longing sweep desolately over her. *I wanted to make you smile. Why wouldn't you let me?* 'Because,' he told her, 'it's been ten years since we last saw each other and, like you said, we are different. A few casual questions could be a start to getting to know you, Noelle.'

'A perfectly understandable assumption, *if* I was here under normal circumstances, wanting to get to know you.'

Despite the coffee and the sunshine and the laptop open on the table, this was not a normal situation. Not remotely, even if for a sorrowful second she wanted it to be. 'You are conveniently forgetting that you kidnapped me—'

'You're not letting me forget it.' His voice had turned hard, reminding her just who she was dealing with.

'Why should I?' Her gaze clashed with his in angry challenge. He looked implacable, standing there, his stony expression giving nothing away. He didn't answer her and she let out a long, low breath. 'Ammar, look. I understand that you went through a very traumatic experience recently, what with the helicopter crash and losing your father. I know that it probably made you think about your life, and maybe wonder or even regret what happened before. About us.' She faltered because, although his expression hadn't changed, he had gone very still—not that unusual for him, really, and yet there was something predatory about that stillness. Something almost frightening. 'And so maybe that's made you think you want…that we should…'

'Get back together?' Ammar filled in softly. She nodded, biting her lip, half-regretting that she'd started down this path. She wasn't sure she believed it, even if it would be convenient to do so. 'Spare me the psychoanalysis, Noelle. That's the last thing I need from you.' He turned away, gazing out of the window at the desert. A lone rock jutted towards the sky, seeming to pierce its hard blueness. 'You were once prepared to spend the rest of your life with me,' he observed, his back still to her, his tone quite detached. 'Can you honestly not spare me a few days now?'

How, Noelle wondered, had he turned the tables on her so neatly? She felt as if she were the one who was being petty and selfish, while *he*—

She took a deep breath. *Focus.* Focus on her goal, which was getting out of here. 'Is that all you want?'

He turned around, his amber eyes seeming to blaze with predatory intent. 'It's a start.'

'What are you saying?'

'Maybe I'll be the one who is Scheherazade in this tale.' She shook her head slowly, not understanding. 'Give me three days,' Ammar explained softly. 'It's Friday. Stay through the weekend at least. You'll have only missed two days of work.'

Noelle felt her heart do a funny sort of flip, a somersault in her chest. Was it from fear—or anticipation? 'And then?' she asked in a low voice.

'And then you can leave me.'

Leave him. It sounded so deliberate, so cold, and yet she'd done it once before. She'd fled from him in the hotel in Rome, and gone back to her family's chateau in Lyon. Her only contact with him after that had been through her father's lawyer, requesting an annulment based on non-consummation of their marriage. He'd signed it and sent it back, and that had been all.

She needed to leave him again. Leave *now.* She should insist on being taken back to Paris right now, this very instant. If she were as strong as she'd thought she was, she would coldly threaten him with lawsuits and litigation. She'd reel off her rights and not back down for one second. But maybe she wasn't that strong after all—as strong as she'd wanted to be—because her single day of defiance had sapped her energy, and even her will.

You loved me once.

Yes, she had, and it was the memory of that love, painful as it was, that made her slowly nod. If she stayed, perhaps she'd get the closure she'd been seeking for so long. And not just closure, but answers. This could be, she knew, her opportunity to finally understand why Ammar had changed after their wedding, what had led him to reject her so humiliatingly and utterly.

Yet did she really want to open that Pandora's box of memories, and the dark tangle of emotions that would surely erupt with it?

Noelle swallowed. She wouldn't answer that yet. She just needed to accept. And her acceptance would be her ticket out of here. 'All right, Ammar, I'll stay until Sunday. But then you're flying me back to Paris, and I'll be back at work by nine a.m. on Monday.'

'I suppose that's fair.'

'Fair?' Noelle heard the bitterness spiking her voice, ten years of bitterness and memories and pain. 'There's nothing fair about it.'

Ammar nodded slowly. 'Perhaps not,' he agreed. 'Life is never very fair.' He turned back to the kitchen counter and stirred something on the stove. 'Come, sit down and eat. You need fattening up.'

'I'm fine the way I am,' Noelle said sharply. She was so prickly. Three days and Ammar probably wouldn't even want to be with her any more. A thought which should have brought relief, and yet irritatingly didn't.

'I agree,' Ammar said in his calm, measured way. 'Perhaps I am the one who needs fattening up.'

Noelle gave a small smile in spite of her every intention to remain composed, even cold. 'You have lost weight,' she remarked, although to her eyes he still looked lithe and powerful, the worn T-shirt hugging the sculpted lines of his chest and shoulders, the faded jeans riding low on his hips. She sat down at the table. 'Was it awful?' she asked quietly. 'The crash?'

Ammar shrugged as he served her a fried egg and several rashers of bacon. She used to love the full fry-up back when she lived in London, but she hadn't had more than black coffee and maybe a croissant for breakfast in years. 'I don't remember much of the actual crash.'

'What happened?'

He sat opposite her with his own plate of eggs and bacon. 'The helicopter engine failed. I don't know why. Perhaps—' He paused, gave a slight shake of his head, and then resumed. 'In any case, we were going down and my father insisted I take the parachute.'

'There was only one?'

'Yes, and I think it was for situations like that one. He wanted to make sure he would be the one to survive.'

She stared at him, horrified. 'But that's…that's criminal!' The word seemed to remain there, suspended, between them.

'My father,' Ammar said quietly, '*was* a criminal.'

Noelle didn't answer. She really didn't want to know just how criminal Balkri Tannous had been. Or his son. Swallowing, she said slowly, 'But he did give it to you.'

'Yes.'

'A change of heart?' She heard the faint note of cynicism in her voice, and knew Ammar heard it, too. He gazed at her sombrely.

'I like to think so. He'd been diagnosed with cancer a few months before. Terminal, and it made him think. Reassess his priorities.'

'Is that what happened to you?' She still sounded cynical.

'I suppose it did. When you're faced with the very real possibility of your own death, you begin to think seriously about what is important.'

Was he actually implying, Noelle wondered, that *she* was important? 'So what happened?' she asked, wanting to keep the conversation focused on facts. 'You parachuted into the sea?'

'Yes, although I don't remember that at all. I hit the water hard and the next thing I knew I was lying on a beach on a tiny deserted island, somewhere, ironically, near Alhaja.' He frowned, his gaze sliding into remembrance. 'My father owns—owned, I should say—all the land in that part of the Mediterranean, and boats steer clear of it. I was lucky to be found at all.'

'And then?'

'Then some poor fishermen took me to the coast of Tunisia, where I battled a fever—from this, I think—' he pointed to the scar on his face '—for several weeks before I finally came to and realised what had happened.'

'And then you came and found me.'

'Yes.'

Noelle stared down at her plate. Somehow, without even realising it, she'd eaten all the bacon and eggs. And she was still hungry. Ammar pushed the toast rack towards her. 'Here.'

Feeling a bit self-conscious, she took a piece of toast and began to butter it. 'And what will you do now? You worked for your father before—'

'Now I will work for myself.' He sounded so flat, so final, and yet strangely triumphant, too.

'As CEO of Tannous Enterprises?'

'Yes.'

'Will it be much different, being the boss?' she asked hesitantly, and Ammar leaned closer to her, his eyes blazing.

'It will be completely different.'

Noelle felt a flare of curiosity but didn't ask any more questions. She shouldn't have asked any questions at all; it suggested an intimacy, a desire for intimacy that she had no intention of feeling.

Or revealing…because she knew then with a rush of regret that she did feel it. She still felt something for Ammar, even if it was only an ember lost in the ashes of their former relationship.

How would she get through the next three days without it fanning into flame? For she knew she was weak and even wanting when it came to him. Already she had started to soften. She rose from the table so quickly she upset her half-drunk cup of coffee. Ammar righted it. Noelle felt her heart beating hard.

'I'm tired. I think I'll go back to my room.'

'Very well.' He rose also, gazing at her calmly.

Noelle stared at him, swallowed the impulse to say something stupid. Something she was afraid she might mean. She'd enjoyed sitting here in the sun talking to him far too much. She'd liked feeling it was possible, or even normal, to be relaxed and open with him.

Swallowing hard, she nodded a jerky farewell and left the room.

Ammar watched Noelle hurry from the kitchen with a pang of frustrated regret. For a few moments there they'd had a normal conversation, and it had felt so easy. Amazingly, wonderfully easy, for he didn't like speaking of the crash or his father or any of his past. His life. Yet how could he win Noelle back if he didn't share any of that? Even he knew enough about love and relationships to understand it couldn't happen in a vacuum of ignorance. Yet sometimes, he acknowledged darkly, ignorance was, if not bliss, then certainly better.

Sighing impatiently, Ammar pushed away from the table. The day stretched emptily in front of him, for he had no doubt Noelle was going to hide in her room for as long as she could. He never should have suggested she stay only through the weekend; he needed a lot longer than three days to convince her to become his wife again. He needed a miracle.

Pushing aside such dark thoughts, he took his laptop and went to his study to work. He closed his eyes briefly at the sight of the endless emails that had landed in his inbox overnight. Everyone wanted to know which way he would turn. If he would follow his father's lead—or his brother's.

In the weeks after the crash, Khalis had taken over Tannous Enterprises, even though their father had disinherited him fifteen years ago, when Khalis had realised the extent of Balkri Tannous's corruption and immorality and walked away. He'd started his own IT firm, made a life for himself in America while Ammar had stayed. Became his father's right-hand man and flunky and carried out all his odious orders. Sold his soul.

Ammar rose from his desk, the regret and anger rushing through him once more. Even before his death, Balkri had wanted to make amends with Khalis. Just as he'd told Noelle, his father's cancer diagnosis had made him long for reconciliation. That, Ammar supposed, had been behind his father secretly signing over the majority of the shares to Khalis just weeks before the crash. Khalis received control of Tannous Enterprises, and as for him?

He would have received nothing, which just showed you shouldn't do deals with the devil. It was only because Khalis didn't want to have anything to do with Tannous Enterprises that Ammar was in charge at all. Yet, now that he was, he longed to make something, not just of himself, but of his father's—*his*—business. Was redemption on such a grand scale even possible?

And as for *personal* redemption… His gut twisted with remorse and even fear. Noelle must wonder what Tannous Enterprises was like, what he had been capable of. What he had done. How could she not, when he'd *kidnapped* her?

Even now, when he wanted to change, to become a good and honest man, he wasn't sure if he could. He wasn't sure he knew how. And if Noelle found out the extent of his deeds, his shame…

There wasn't a chance in hell—where he surely belonged—of her staying.

CHAPTER FOUR

NOELLE stayed in her room for two hours before she decided she was being ridiculous. She couldn't hide up here for ever. Besides, it was boring. And, amazingly, she was getting hungry again. But, more than either of those, she wanted to see Ammar. It was time, she decided, for some answers.

She left the confines of her bedroom and went in search of him. The house was so very quiet and she hadn't even heard the sound of another voice or step. Did Ammar have any staff, or were they completely alone? She peeked in the kitchen, saw their breakfast dishes had been cleared away, the room tidied. But Ammar—or anyone else—was nowhere in sight.

She tiptoed down the main hallway, looked in a living room, dining room and—surprisingly—a music room with a very good grand piano, but all were empty.

Where was he?

'Are you looking for me?'

Noelle whirled around and saw Ammar standing in a doorway that had been made to look like part of the wall, so cleverly disguised she hadn't even seen it. And he'd been so quiet. As quiet as a cat, or a thief.

She swallowed, nodded. 'Yes. I wanted to talk to you.'

'That makes for a pleasant change.' He turned to close

the door behind him. With it shut, Noelle couldn't make it out at all.

'Why the secret door?' she asked.

'I possess a great deal of highly classified information.' She didn't ask anything more. 'Shall we go outside? It's not too hot in the garden.'

'There's a garden? I didn't see one from my window.'

'It's on the other side of the house.' He led her through the music room, past the piano to a pair of French windows that led out to an enclosed garden with a seating area and an infinity pool shaded by palms. The trees and shrubs—as well as the high walls—provided some shelter from the desert wind and sun.

'Do you play piano?' Noelle asked and Ammar nodded. 'I didn't know that. Did you…did you play when we were…together?'

Another nod. 'It's not something I usually tell people.'

'Why not?'

He shrugged. 'A private thing, I suppose, music.'

She stared at him, standing across from her in the little flower-scented enclave, looking calm but also tense, even a little resigned. He dug his hands into the pockets of his jeans and waited, as though for a verdict. 'I don't really know you,' she said quietly, 'at all.'

'I know.'

Strange, but she hadn't expected that admission. It made her sad. She took a deep breath, let it out slowly. 'I want some answers.' Ammar nodded. Waited. Noelle made herself ask, 'Why…why did you reject me? In the hotel?' Now the words were out there, she wished she could unsay them. Did she really want to hear how he'd changed his mind, how he'd no longer been attracted to her, had never been attracted to her? Why else would a husband refuse to have sex with his wife?

'I suppose,' Ammar said carefully, 'it felt like the only choice at the time.'

'Why?'

He said nothing. Frustration bubbled up inside her; she might as well be staring at a stone wall. 'Ammar, if you have any hope of a relationship with me, surely you realise I need some real answers? There can be no relationship without honesty.'

'It's not that simple.'

'It *is*.'

Frustration flared in his eyes, lighting them with its fire. 'You are viewing the world like a child—'

'I am *not* a child!' That stung, because she knew how naive and innocent she'd once been, believing the best of him, of *them*, even after all hope was gone. She wasn't that woman—that silly girl—any more. 'I think most people would agree that honesty is essential in *any* relationship.'

'I am not denying that,' Ammar said tightly. 'But I am not sure how much honesty I am willing to give—or you are willing to hear.'

Suddenly she was silenced. He was right. Just how honest did she actually want him to be? And why was she arguing about the necessity of it when she had no intention of having any sort of relationship with him? Still, she needed to know. Something, no matter how small. She let out a shuddering breath.

'Our wedding night—I was lying in bed waiting for you and the doorknob turned, as if someone was about to come in. Was it you?'

A beat passed, the only sound the whisper of the wind, the gentle lap of the water in the pool. 'Yes.'

She let out another rush of breath. 'Were you going to come in, and then you changed your mind?'

'Yes.'

'*Why?*'

'Because…' He stopped, lifting a hand as if to rake it through his hair before he remembered he hardly had any any more. He dropped it to his side, turning away from her with an impatient hiss of breath.

'Ammar—'

'This is not easy for me, Noelle.'

Again she was silenced. She had assumed, she realised, that it *was* easy. Or, if not exactly easy, then a matter of little consequence. Long ago, in her own hurt and humiliation, she'd decided he had never actually cared about her one way or the other. She had been, it seemed, a matter of indifference to him. Yet the man standing across from her, radiating an angry tension, his whole body taut and pulsating with it, was not indifferent to her. Not remotely.

'I don't understand.'

'I know.' He turned back to her, his body now rigid with resolve. 'I didn't come to you that night—or any night— because I thought it would be easier for you.'

'*Easier?*'

'Not to be married to me.'

She stared at him, her mind whirling with this revelation. She had imagined many painful reasons why Ammar had rejected her. He was tired of her, he'd changed his mind, he'd never really loved her to begin with. She had never imagined this. 'Easier,' she repeated in disbelief, 'for me.'

'Yes.'

'*How?*'

His mouth tightened and his jaw worked but no words came. Finally, with effort, he said, 'I realised our marriage wouldn't work, and so I was offering you a way out.'

She shook her head, refusing to believe so simplistic, so *ridiculous* an explanation. 'But you never said anything,

Ammar. You…you acted as though you couldn't bear to be with me for a single second.' Just the memory made her throat tighten and she blinked hard.

'That wasn't the case.'

'And I'm supposed to believe that?'

'It's the truth.'

She shook her head so hard her vision blurred. *'No.* You're rewriting history, Ammar, or maybe you're lying—'

'I am not,' Ammar said coldly, 'lying.'

'How am I supposed to believe any of that?' Noelle burst out. 'How am I supposed to believe you were actually doing me a favour when you treated me like you hated me?'

Ammar's mouth tightened. 'I've had enough of this conversation.'

'Well, I haven't—'

'All you need to know—' he cut across her '—is that I realised it wasn't going to work, and I meant to let you go.'

'Let me *go*? That's your version of events? Because it sure as hell is different from mine. You weren't letting me go, Ammar, you were letting me down.' Her throat ached and her eyes stung even as anger blazed through her. 'So, just like that, you were willing to give up on our marriage, on *me*, without even a word of explanation, before we'd even begun?' It hurt, even now. Especially now, because somehow the truth was worse than anything Noelle could have imagined. It made the loss and grief fresh again, and so very raw.

'I wasn't giving up on you,' Ammar said quietly. 'I was giving up on me.'

She stared at him, his words seeming to echo through her. She could find no hint in his expressionless face as to what he'd felt then—and what he felt now. 'What do you mean?'

Another long silence. Ammar's face looked as if it had

been harshly hewn from stone. 'I knew I couldn't be the husband you deserved.'

She forced herself to ignore the ache his words—and the quiet, sad tone in which he said them—gave her. 'Why not?' Ammar's expression closed down, if that were even possible. It wasn't as if he'd been an open book to begin with. It wasn't, Noelle reflected bitterly, as if he'd been open about anything at all. 'I still feel like I don't understand anything,' she said, her voice caught between exasperation and something darker and far more alarming. It shouldn't even matter now, the reasons why, and yet Noelle knew from the misery swamping her, the heartache that felt as if it were rending her right in two, that it did. It mattered far too much.

'I realised I'd been fooling myself,' Ammar said flatly, 'all along. It wouldn't work between us and I didn't want to drag you down. That's why I walked away.'

His words fell into the taut stillness. 'And you just happened to decide that, right after we got married?' Noelle struggled to hold onto her anger instead of giving into the desolation that threatened to sweep right through her. 'You couldn't have figured that out before? You couldn't have told me, *talked* to me—'

'What's done is done,' Ammar said flatly, and Noelle let out a choked cry that sounded far too like a sob.

'But it isn't done for me, Ammar. It's *never* been done. Why else would I be here demanding answers? Why would you even want me to be here? And how has it changed now? How have *you* changed?' His jaw tightened. He said nothing. '*Is* it different?' she demanded. 'Why do you think a marriage between us could work now, when you didn't think it could before?' She took a step towards him, her fists clenched. She felt so angry, ridiculously angry, considering what ancient history this was. Should be. 'You're not telling me the truth, are you? Not the whole truth.'

'I'm telling you enough.'

'By whose say-so? All I know is that you changed your mind and so you abandoned me. Well, guess what, Ammar. I knew that before.'

'It wasn't like that, Noelle.' For the first time he raised his voice and anger flashed in his eyes like lightning.

'It *felt* like that.' She let out a ragged breath, felt tears sting her eyes. 'It took me years to get over our marriage, Ammar, to get over you, and all because you couldn't bother to tell me what was really going on. You *still* can't.'

'I'm sorry.' He took a breath, let it out slowly. 'I'm sorry,' he said again, and even though his voice was flat and hard she knew he meant it.

'Why?' she whispered. 'Why, really?'

'I was living in a dream world, those days with you,' Ammar said quietly. 'And on our wedding night, I woke up.'

'How?'

He shook his head. 'It doesn't matter.'

It did matter, of course it did, but this time Noelle didn't press. Her anger had deserted her, leaving her as emotionally exposed as she'd been that horrible night in the hotel, when he'd thrust her away from him.

Ammar still looked completely expressionless, stony and blank, and belatedly she realised she had tears running down her face. Perfect. So much for being strong and independent, needing no one. Twenty-four hours with Ammar and she was a pathetic mess. He still hadn't spoken, hadn't even moved, and Noelle had no idea what he was thinking. She felt more confused than ever before. With a revealingly loud sniff, she turned on her heel and walked quickly out of the garden.

Unfortunately there wasn't anywhere to go except back up to her bedroom. She couldn't exactly take a stroll through the Sahara. She paced the room, alternating between anger and desolation, until finally, exhausted, she fell onto her bed and cried in earnest, her tears muffled by the pillow. It felt good to cry, a needed release, and yet she still hated that she was crying about Ammar, a *decade* after their marriage had ended. Did you ever really move on? Time was supposed to heal all wounds, but the ones on her heart felt as red and raw as the scar on Ammar's face.

Eventually she fell into a restless doze and when she woke the setting sun was casting long shadows on the floor of her room and someone was knocking on her door.

She struggled up, swiping her tangled hair away from her face. 'Yes?' she called, her voice sounding croaky.

'Dinner is served, *mademoiselle.*'

Noelle didn't recognise the woman's voice, but she assumed she was some kind of household staff. So she and Ammar weren't alone here. 'Thank you,' she called, and rose from the bed.

What now? she wondered dully. What would she say to Ammar when she saw him again? How would she even manage to keep herself together? She still had forty-eight hours to endure in this desert prison. Two days left with Ammar.

As she changed into a pale blue linen sheath—again too big, so she cinched it with a wide belt—his words, his tone, even the sombre expression on his face all came back in a heart-rending wave of anguish.

I wasn't giving up on you. I was giving up on me. I knew I couldn't be the husband you deserved.

Noelle sank onto a cushioned stool in front of the dressing table and dropped her face into her hands. She wasn't angry any more, she realised with a pang of regret. Anger was easier, but now she felt only an overwhelming sadness for what had been…and what hadn't been. What could have been, if only Ammar had been honest with her back when they'd been married.

Are you sure about that? a voice in her head, sly and insidious, mocked. *Do you really want to know why he thought he couldn't be a husband to you, the kind of husband you deserved?*

Did it even matter?

She lifted her head from her hands and stared at her reflection in the mirror. Her face was pale, her eyes huge and dark with deep violet shadows underneath them. *Did* it matter? Was her heart, even now, contemplating some kind of future with Ammar, even as her mind insisted she would be leaving in two days? Her heart was ever deceitful and she knew, with a sudden stark clarity, that this was why she had been so emotionally volatile since she'd first laid eyes on him.

She was afraid she still loved him, or at least *could* love him, if she let herself.

Yet how could you love someone you'd never really known?

She drew in a deep breath and let it out slowly. She had no answer to that one.

Ammar rose from the table as soon as Noelle entered the room. She looked pale but composed, the blue sheath dress emphasising the slenderness of her body, the sharp angle of her collarbone, and making her seem fragile. He felt a powerful surge of protectiveness, even as he acknowledged how useless it was. Noelle didn't need his protection now. She didn't want it.

All afternoon her scathing indictment of his actions had

reverberated through him, a remorseless echo he could neither ignore nor deny.

It took me years to get over our marriage, Ammar, to get over you, and all because you couldn't bother to tell me what was really going on. You still can't.

No, he couldn't. He didn't yet possess the courage or strength to tell her the whole truth. He didn't know if he ever would, even as he bleakly acknowledged that Noelle would keep demanding answers. Wanting to know all his secrets—secrets that could only hurt them both.

And he'd hurt her too much already. He had never, he realised, considered that he'd acted selfishly by walking away from Noelle. If he were honest with himself, which he had been, painfully, that afternoon, he'd attributed a kind of self-sacrificing nobility to his actions, considered it one of the better things he had done in his sorry life.

What a joke. What a *tragedy*.

'Ammar?'

He focused on her now, saw how she placed her hand on her throat, her pulse fluttering underneath her fingertips. She was nervous. Was she *afraid*? The thought that she might actually be frightened of him was unbearable.

'I'm sorry,' he said, starting forward. 'I was lost in thought. Come, sit down.' He reached for her hand, surprised and gratified when she took it. Just the feel of her slender fingers in his caused a shaft of longing to pierce him with its impossible sweetness. He wanted her so much. He'd always wanted her, longed for her with a desperation that had scared him, and yet he'd let her believe he didn't desire her at all, never truly considering the pain it would cause her. Never wanting to. That was how he'd survived working for his father for so long. *Don't think about what you're doing. Don't think about the pain you cause. Don't think at all.*

She sat down, slipping her hand from his and reaching for her napkin. After a second's silence she looked up at him, her eyes so wide and dark. 'I don't know what to say to you.'

'That makes two of us.' He served her some *kousksi bil djaj*, a Tunisian speciality with chicken and couscous.

While they were eating, he searched for an innocuous topic of conversation. 'Tell me about Arche.'

'Arche?'

'That was the name of the shop you work for? What do you do exactly?'

'Oh. Yes.' She looked a little startled that he would remember, that he would ask. 'I buy accessories and footwear for the women's department.'

'And what does that entail?' He wasn't all that interested in women's shoes, but he liked to listen to Noelle. He enjoyed the way her cheeks flushed petal-pink and her eyes lit from within, turning them almost golden. And they both needed a relief from the intensity of their earlier conversation. God knew he did.

'I go to all the fashion shows, decide what's going to be popular each season. Keep an eye on what people are wearing. A lot of it is about predicting trends.'

'That can be a bit of a gamble.'

'Yes...' She gave a little laugh. 'I predicted that faux-fur ankle boots were going to be big one winter and they were a complete flop. To be honest, I didn't even like them. They made you look like you had hairy feet.'

She made a face and he smiled, felt himself lighten, just a little bit, inside. 'Not exactly the look one attempts, I imagine.'

'No, indeed. I bought a pair and wore them for a season, though.' She lifted her shoulders in a shrug. 'All part of the job.'

'I think you could probably pull them off,' he said, and saw her flush deepen. He felt a fierce dart of possessive satisfaction that she still reacted to him, still maybe, miraculously wanted him. 'You'd look good in just about anything.'

She froze and something flashed in her eyes. 'Not, it seems,' she said, her voice tight, 'a silk teddy and stilettos.'

Shock iced through him. She was, of course, talking about that night in the hotel. That wretched, wretched night when she'd thrown herself at him and he'd pushed her away, both for her own protection and his. He took a steadying sip of wine. 'So what was one of your accurate predictions?'

Her mouth tightened and she looked away. 'Grey being the new black, I suppose,' she finally said, and he felt a rush of relief. She wasn't going to press.

'You seem to favour dark colours now.' She'd worn black when he'd seen her at the charity ball, and grey the day after.

'Dark colours are trendy at the moment,' she said flatly. 'And I need to stay with the trends.'

'I liked seeing you in bright colours.'

She gave him a sharp look. 'I'm different now, Ammar. I know you think we can somehow pick up where we left off—not that I'd even want to, but in any case we can't. I'm a completely different person.'

And she was intent on reminding him at every opportunity. Funny, how he was the one trying to make small talk now. It had always been Noelle before, drawing him out with her jokes and laughter, her innocent chatter. He'd loved it, even if he hadn't always known how to respond. 'How?' he asked as mildly as he could. Deliberately he arched an eyebrow, managed something he hoped was close to a smile.

She stared at him. 'How?'

'Yes, how. How are you so different?' He genuinely wanted to know. 'How have you changed?'

She narrowed her gaze. 'I'm not as naïve as I once was. Or as innocent. And I don't believe in fairy tale happy endings, either.' Every statement sounded like an accusation, a judgement. Ammar glanced away.

'I see,' he said quietly.

'And how have you changed?' she asked, a strident note of challenge in her voice. Ammar felt that familiar flare of anger. She sounded mocking, like she didn't believe he had changed. That he could.

'Well, there's this.' He gestured to the scar on his face. 'And I'm thinking about keeping my hair short. They cut it all off when I was feverish—I suppose it was filthy. But I'm finding it very easy to manage.'

She stared at him and he knew she was torn between a sudden, surprised amusement and a deeper frustration. 'You know that's not what I mean.'

'Somehow,' he said, his voice now carrying an edge even he heard, 'I don't feel like baring my soul to you when you look like you want to bite my head off.'

'You've *never* bared your soul to me. You've never shared anything with me.'

He felt his fingers clench into an involuntary fist. 'It didn't feel that way this afternoon.'

Noelle gave a snort of disbelief. His fist tightened, his fingers aching. 'You call that baring your soul? Ammar, you were speaking in riddles, telling me you realised it wouldn't work and you meant to let me go, blah, blah, blah. Vague nonsense. I still don't understand anything. Understand you.'

'Maybe,' he said, his teeth gritted, 'I don't want to be understood.'

'Then what do you want?' she demanded, her voice rising in both challenge and frustration. 'Because you told me you wanted to restore our marriage, to be *husband and wife*, but I don't even know what that means. It obviously doesn't mean honesty, because getting a straight answer from you is like pulling teeth. It doesn't mean closeness, because you've been keeping your distance in just about every way possible. So what? A warm body in your bed?' She smacked her forehead, rolling her eyes, and a blind rage pulsed through him. 'Oh, no, never that, because you have *never* wanted me in your bed.'

'Don't,' he said in a low voice.

'Don't what? Don't speak the truth? Why not? What do I have to lose? You've already kidnapped me, refused to let me go—'

'You're never going to forget that—'

'Why should I? Why on earth should I come back to you? I loved you ten years ago, yes, but you were different—'

'I wasn't different,' Ammar cut across her. 'When I was with you, I was the man I wanted to be.'

She stared at him, clearly stunned into silence by an admission he hadn't meant to make. The silence stretched on between them, endless and exposing. He felt as if she'd turned a spotlight on his soul. 'And now?' she finally whispered.

His throat ached, the words drawn from him so reluctantly, yet he knew he had to say them. She needed to hear them. 'I want to be that man again.'

She said nothing, but Ammar saw the sorrow in her eyes, turning them dark, and she gave a little shake of her head. He rose from the table. He'd had enough. Enough of this awful intimacy, of feeling so exposed. Enough of her accusations and judgement. 'Enough,' he said out loud, his voice hard and flat. 'We have discussed this enough.'

'We haven't even begun—'

'I am finished.' He threw his napkin on the table as he turned away from her. 'I will arrange for my helicopter to transport you to Marrakech. You can leave tonight.'

Noelle watched Ammar walk from the room with long, angry strides with a sense of incredulity. Leave tonight? He was letting her go, then. He'd given up. She was free.

So why, sitting there alone, did she not feel jubilant? Or at least relieved? Amazingly, aggravatingly, she felt worse than ever. Carefully Noelle folded her napkin and laid it on the table. The house was as still and silent as always; did Ammar ever make any noise? Where had he gone?

He'd been furious, she knew that. She'd made him angry, and she saw now she'd done it on purpose because she was afraid. Afraid of giving in and letting herself feel anything for him again. So she'd pushed and pushed, asking for answers but really driving him away. And yet, now that she had, she wished she hadn't. She wished…what?

She was afraid to acknowledge what she wished for. So afraid. She shouldn't even be asking herself these kinds of questions. What she should do, Noelle knew, was walk right out of here. She'd get on the helicopter to Marrakech, a plane to Paris. She'd never see Ammar again.

The thought gave her a piercing pain, a direct stab to the heart. She didn't want that. She closed her eyes, pressed the heels of her hands hard against her sockets. Why couldn't she want that? Why couldn't she be strong enough to walk away?

What about being strong enough to stay?

That thought felt like a thunderbolt from the sky, striking her heart, splintering her convictions. What was she thinking? Wanting?

I don't want to leave yet. I don't know what that means, what hope there is for us, but I don't want to leave.

But what would happen if she stayed?

She felt her stomach hollow out and adrenalin course through her veins. Her heart began to thud with both anticipation and fear. Terror, really, because to contemplate such a thing would be to open herself up to the kind of devastating pain and heartache she had felt once before, and had since arranged her whole life to never feel again.

How could she even think of it?

How could she not?

Slowly Noelle rose from the table. Her heart was beating so hard and fast now it felt like a drumming through her body, an ocean roaring in her ears. Her legs were weak and wobbly as she walked from the room. She was going to find Ammar.

And then?

Slowly she walked through each empty room. She even found the disguised door and peeked in the study, surprisingly unlocked, but he was not there. She saw papers scattered on his desk, an open laptop, and turned away. In the music room she saw the French windows were ajar and she knew he must be outside, in the garden. With her fingertips she pushed the door open wider and stepped out into the night.

It was completely dark except for a swathe of light given by a sliver of moon, and it took her several moments to see enough to put one foot in front of the other. The little seating area where they'd spoken earlier was empty, but she saw a narrow stone path winding its way between the flowers and shrubs and she took it. She felt as if her heart, with its relentless pounding, was leading her onwards. Her heart, trembling thing that it was, would guide both her steps and words.

The path led to a private courtyard, with one wrought iron little bench. It was a pretty little space, or Noelle imagined it would be in daylight. Her breath caught in her chest and her heart beat harder as she saw Ammar sitting on the bench, his shoulders bowed, his head in his hands.

In the distance she heard the sound of an engine coughing to life, the whirr of propellers. So he really did expect her to leave. And she should leave, if she wanted to stay safe. Strong. It was so obvious, and yet…

She took a step towards him. He looked up and in the darkness she could not make out his expression at all, yet she felt his desperation and hunger like a palpable thing; it was the same thing she was feeling.

'I don't want to go,' she said, her voice little more than a croak. She cleared her throat, forced herself to sound stronger. To feel it. 'I want to stay.'

CHAPTER FIVE

AMMAR didn't answer. For one endless charged moment the silence strained between them and Noelle braced herself for yet another awful rejection. What had she been thinking, risking herself again? Opening herself up to all sorts of pain?

Then in one fluid movement he rose from the bench and crossed to her. Noelle didn't have time to respond or even think as he took her in his arms and kissed her with a passionate force that thrilled her to her core.

His lips captured hers, hungry, demanding, relentless. Her mouth parted and her hands clutched his shoulders, drawing him closer. She'd needed this. Craved it, for it was only with Ammar that she felt her body and heart open up, everything in her reaching for him, pleading...

And then he pulled away, just a little, yet still leaving her bereft. He rested his forehead against hers, just as he had the first time he'd kissed her, his breath coming out in a shudder. Noelle tensed; it felt like an apology, a rejection. Trying not to tremble, she stepped away from him.

'I don't mean... I'm not saying... You still *kidnapped* me,' she said, the words both a warning and an accusation. A way to protect herself.

Ammar didn't move, and yet she felt as if something

had left him, something inside him had suddenly winked out. 'I see,' he said quietly, and she bit her lip, forced herself not to say anything more. To apologise. The silence stretched on.

She could not, Noelle thought, have doused their earlier passion more effectively or completely if she'd poured ice water over the pair of them. Ammar might have stopped the kiss, but she'd ruined the mood. It was just as well. She wasn't ready to risk that much with Ammar. She wasn't ready to risk rejection again. Even now she remembered how he'd thrust her away from him when she'd tried to make him want her that horrible evening in the hotel. Clad in her ridiculous teddy and stilettos—the clothes of a seductress, a whore—she'd asked brokenly, *Don't you want me?*

She'd never forget his answer.

No. No, I don't. Just leave me, Noelle. Get out of here.

And so she had, shaking with the pain of it, a pain so great she felt as if her body could not hold it. He didn't love her. Didn't want her the way a man wanted a woman, the way a husband should want a wife.

And now with that memory came doubt, treacherous, terrible, seeping into her heart like some noxious gas, a deadly poison. Why had she told him she'd stay, that she *wanted* to stay? She drew a shuddering breath and backed away.

'I think I should—'

'Don't.' Ammar cut her off quietly, yet with certain purpose. 'Don't leave. Please.'

It was, stupidly, the please that got her. He'd tacked it on as an afterthought, yet sincerity throbbed in his voice. *I want to be that man again.* He was trying to change.

She took another deep breath. 'I won't leave tonight,' she said, the implication clear. *But I might tomorrow.* He wouldn't stop her now, she knew. This was her choice. 'But if you want us to have any chance of making something between us work, then you…you have to *try*.'

'I know,' Ammar said, his voice so low it seemed to re-verberate right through her. 'I know.'

The silence stretched between them. Noelle didn't know what to say. She felt too raw and vulnerable to reassure him; she was half-regretting her agreement to stay the night already. Yet when Ammar turned to look at her, she saw the longing and hunger in his eyes and everything inside her twisted in a confusing mixture of hope and re-gret. Without another word she turned and walked out of the garden.

She was exhausted but she couldn't sleep. She felt an unsettling clash of hope and despair, her emotions veer-ing from one to the other. She asked herself what on earth she was doing here, staying with a man who had broken both her heart and the law. She should leave, get out while she could.

And while the stronger, harder self she had cultivated over the last ten years insisted that she tell Ammar to re-lease her in the morning, the quiet voice of her heart whis-pered that she'd never really wanted to be that person in the first place.

That quiet voice became more insistent, telling her that he was the only man who had reached her, touched her soul and her heart. Yet did he love her? He'd never said. Ten years ago she'd assumed he did, naively, trustingly, because she didn't think he could look at her the way he did, or brush her hair, or cup her cheek, and not love her. Yet now she was different and she no longer believed in the simple boy-meets-girl fantasy. She didn't trust happy end-ings, had deliberately let go of the dreams she'd once cher-ished. The little house, a family, a husband. She didn't want those things any longer. So why was she here? Why had she stayed and told herself—and him—that she would try?

Because, Noelle knew with an appalling certainty, she wanted to believe. Even now, when absolutely everything seemed stacked against them, when their past history and hurt were proof positive that faith in love and happy-ever-afters was not just naïve but delusional, she wanted to believe.

How stupid, she thought with a weary bitterness, was that?

She must have slept because she awoke suddenly, blinking in the darkness. The clock read a little after two in the morning. In the distance she heard the sound of someone playing the piano; after a moment she recognised the haunting melody as *Pathétique*, Beethoven's melancholy Eighth Sonata. Silently she slipped from the bed and, dressed only in a silky nightie that fell to her knees, she headed downstairs.

The whole house was quiet and still, except for the sound of the piano. Noelle paused on the threshold of the music room, the door only a little ajar, the sorrowful sound of the music sweeping through her. She was no expert, but she could recognise when someone played with both talent and passion. Ammar was such a man.

Quietly she stepped into the room. He was so absorbed in his playing that he didn't notice her and she watched him for a moment. He wore only a pair of loose drawstring trousers; his chest was bare and glorious, all taut, sleek muscle, although she could see some faded bruises from the crash on his back. His long, lean fingers moved elegantly over the keys, evoking a sound filled with such loss and longing that Noelle fought the urge to cross the room and put her arms around him.

Perhaps she made some sound, for Ammar suddenly

looked over at her and his hands stilled on the keys, plunging the room into silence.

'You play so beautifully,' Noelle said after a moment. 'Why didn't you ever tell me you played piano?' Inwardly, she flinched. It sounded like an accusation.

Ammar played a few single discordant notes. 'I didn't tell anyone,' he said after a moment. 'It's always been a very private thing.'

She took a step into the room. The only light came from a single lamp on top of the piano; it cast its warm yellow glow over Ammar's lowered head. 'You must have had lessons, though.' He shook his head. 'You mean you taught yourself?'

'At boarding school. I used to sneak into the music room after hours.' His mouth twisted in a grimace that Noelle thought he meant to seem wry but wasn't. 'Breaking the law.'

'It was certainly justified,' she said as lightly as she could, 'if you play like that.'

He played a minor chord, the mournful notes echoing in the stillness of the room. 'Is it ever justified?'

She knew he was talking about more than just breaking into a music room. *I've done too many things already I could be arrested for.* She wasn't ready to think about that, much less hear it from him. *Coward,* she berated herself. She remained silent, half in the room, her hesitation obvious. Ammar glanced up at her, his narrowed, knowing eyes taking in everything about her. She wasn't fooling him. She wasn't fooling him at all.

Swallowing, she took a step closer. 'Why did you have to sneak into the music room at school?' she asked. 'Couldn't you have had proper lessons?'

'My father forbade it.'

'Why?'

A shrug. 'Music was useless, I suppose, to him.' He took a breath, let it out slowly. 'My father had very definite ideas about what a man should be like. What he should do, or even think.'

'Your father,' she said, taking a step closer to him, 'has a lot to answer for.'

'You have no idea.'

Ammar's voice was so low and grim that Noelle flinched from it. 'I know I don't,' she said softly, and for several moments neither of them said anything more. 'So how did you decide you wanted to play the piano anyway?' she finally asked. 'If you'd never played before?'

'My mother played. She was a professional and she might have had a great career, but she gave it all up when she married my father.'

'I suppose she thought it was worth it,' Noelle said uncertainly.

Ammar gave a little shake of his head. 'She had no choice.'

'What do you mean?'

'My father insisted upon it. No wife of his would ever work, or be seen needing to work.'

'And your mother accepted it?'

'She was in love with him, or at least she thought she was.' He played another minor chord. 'Perhaps she didn't really know him.'

Noelle felt a shiver of unease. Was Ammar talking about his parents, or about them? And surely, surely he was different from Balkri Tannous. She had to believe that. Deliberately she moved forward and sat next to him on the piano bench. Surprised, he shifted over to give her more room, but even so their thighs brushed against one another and Noelle felt a bolt of awareness at the contact.

'Did you ever play the piano?' he asked.

'I took lessons for a few months when I was about eight. My parents made me.' She lifted her shoulders in a shrug, the gesture an apology. 'I didn't like it and so I didn't practise and eventually they let me stop.' She was uncomfortably and even painfully aware of the differences in their situations, in their very selves: Ammar had had to sneak into a music room to learn an instrument he loved, while she'd been given it freely and scorned it.

'You could learn now,' he said and, to her surprise, he took her hands and placed them on the piano keys, his own hands large and warm over hers. She stared at their twined hands, his skin callused and brown, her fingers slender and soft, the colour of cream. They were so different, she thought, in so many ways.

Carefully, Ammar pressed her hands down on certain keys. 'C, C, A, A, G,' he recited quietly, pressing each of her fingers down in turn.

Mesmerised by the simple touch of his hands on hers, Noelle could not recognise the tune for a moment. She felt as if a fist had plunged into the centre of her chest and grabbed hold of her heart. Squeezed. She was breathless with both longing and loss, and even a faint, frail joy.

'F, F, E, E,' Ammar continued, and she finally turned to him with a small smile.

'Twinkle, Twinkle, Little Star.'

'You know it.' He smiled back at her faintly, his lips barely curving but, even so, Noelle felt her already squeezed heart give a painful little lurch. He looked so beautiful and so sad, and she felt so much in that moment she couldn't speak. He reached up and gently touched her cheek with the tips of his fingers. She closed her eyes. 'You're so beautiful,' he said, his voice so low that, even seated next to him, she had to strain to hear it. 'So very lovely. I've always thought that.'

She drew in a shuddering breath. 'I think I've always known you did.'

'Have you?' He sounded more sad than surprised.

'Yes.' She knew she was speaking the truth. She still didn't understand why Ammar had rejected her during their brief marriage, but she knew he'd felt something for her, both then and now. He cared. He'd always cared.

Gently she placed her hand over his, pressing it against her cheek. She opened her eyes. 'Ammar—' Her throat was so tight it hurt to get the words out. 'Won't you tell me why...why you turned away from me? You said you didn't come to me on our wedding night because you meant to let me go, but...' She trailed off, not wanting to put it into words. Still Ammar said nothing. She drew in another breath. 'I still don't understand. I still feel like you're hiding something from me, like...like you don't want me.'

Still no words. He'd gone completely still, his face utterly expressionless. Noelle searched his face, longing for just one clue to what he was feeling. What he was hiding. 'Ammar?' she prompted, and now her voice wobbled.

He looked away, dropping his hand from her cheek. Sitting next to him, she could feel the tension steal through his body, the hand that had touched her so tenderly now clenched into a fist. 'I want you to know,' he said in a low voice, so low she felt it reverberate right through her chest, 'that I have always wanted you. Desired you. I still do.' He paused, his whole body angled away from her now, even though they were only inches apart. 'Desperately.'

Desperately. The knowledge might have thrilled her once, but now she felt only a weary—and wary—confusion. 'Why then have you never...?' She broke off as in one abrupt movement Ammar rose from the piano bench and crossed the room, his back to her.

Away from the lamp that provided the only light in the

room, he was swathed in shadow. In the half-darkness
Noelle could still see the sinuous muscles of his back, the
faded bruises from the crash.

'Can't that be enough?' he asked, his voice raw. 'Can't
you be satisfied with that?'

He sounded so tired, so tormented that Noelle almost
wanted to agree. But what kind of future could they possibly have with so many secrets between them? 'No,' she
said quietly, 'I can't.'

Ammar let out a shuddering breath. 'What I told you
was true. I didn't come to you on our wedding night because I knew I had to let you go. But you're right. There
was more to it than that.'

Noelle held her breath, waiting, always waiting.
'Ammar—'

'It wasn't your fault,' he said quietly. 'I don't want you
ever to feel like I was rejecting you.'

'But you were,' Noelle protested, and he shook his head,
the movement abrupt and almost violent.

'*No.* Never. Never that.' He turned around and the agony
written on his face was almost too painful to see. A lump
rose in her throat and she felt fear beat its relentless tattoo through her veins. What terrible thing was he going to
tell her? Could she bear it? Would it change everything?

'It's late,' he said, and she saw his expression close once
more, agony turned into adamance. She would get no more
answers tonight. 'We'll talk tomorrow,' he said. 'I…I want
to spend time with you, just being with you, before I…' He
shook his head, closed his eyes briefly. 'Please.'

'All right,' she whispered. She knew it was futile to
press him now. His eyes were dark, his face hard, his
body rigid. And maybe she had heard enough, for tonight
at least.

'Come,' he said, and reached for her hand. Surprised,

Noelle let him thread his fingers through hers and lead her from the room. All around them the house was dark and still, the only sound the tread of their bare feet upon the tiles. Ammar led her up the stairs, down a corridor and past her own bedroom. Her heart lurched. Her breath hitched.

What—?

Outside a closed door, he turned to her, touched her cheek. 'Sleep with me,' he said, 'in my bed.'

Such a simple request, Noelle thought, and yet she knew it cost him. His eyes were dark and intent, his body still rigid with tension. She smiled, although she felt it wobble.

'Yes,' she said, and followed him into his bedroom.

CHAPTER SIX

AMMAR led Noelle into the darkness of his own bedroom, to the king-sized bed with its rumpled duvet. He hesitated, wanting so much to be with her and yet…

He'd never spent an entire night with a woman before. Even now, just the thought made him tense, panic. He hated the duality of his own desires, the longing to draw her close even as memories reared up and demanded he keep his distance.

'Ammar?' She placed one slender hand on his shoulder, her touch cool and soft. With effort he turned to her and smiled. At least he hoped he did. His mouth curved, at least. The moonlight, he saw, streamed over her, turning her skin luminescent. Her chestnut hair tumbled down her back in artless waves and her eyes were wide and trusting. Even now, when he'd demanded and denied and become angry, she trusted him. She followed him and waited with a patience that felt unbearably gentle. He was humbled, but he was also afraid.

He never let women close. They never spent the night, they never touched his heart. Only Noelle had succeeded, and in fear—both for her and, yes, for himself—he'd walked away all those years ago. Could he stay now? Could he finally put the ghosts of his past, the mistakes and sins and endless regrets, to rest? She reached up and cupped his palm with her cheek.

'I don't have to stay.'

Ammar felt his throat tighten so it hurt to speak. 'I want you to.' He knew he sounded grudging. Why, even now, did it have to be so difficult?

Noelle reached past him and pulled the duvet back. 'Well,' she said, smiling a little, 'it's freezing in here so I think I'll get under the covers.'

He watched in a sort of dazed incredulity as she got in the bed and scooted to one side, pulling the duvet up to her chin. She looked so right there, he thought, in his bed. That was the most incredible thing of all.

'There's plenty of room,' she told him, her expression almost mischievous over the edge of the duvet. He loved that even now she could tease. How much was it costing her?

Ammar got in the bed, feeling wooden and awkward as he stretched out next to her. He desperately wanted this to be normal, but he didn't know how to act. What to feel. Surely not this blind panic that fell over him like a fog, memories shrieking inside him.

Sleep. They were meant to sleep. Ammar closed his eyes. Belatedly, he realised he should touch her, he *wanted* to touch her, so he laid one hand on her shoulder. He felt that shoulder shake and he tensed.

'What?'

'Ammar, you're acting like...like you're at the dentist or something.' He realised she was actually laughing, just a little, although underneath he sensed her confusion and hurt. He froze, unsure again how to feel. Anger felt more familiar, yet he struggled against it. He didn't want to feel it, to ruin the moment, awkward as it already was.

Then she rolled over to face him and placed her palms, so warm and soft, on his bare chest. 'Come here,' she whispered and, strangely, miraculously, it felt like the simplest and most natural thing in the world to pull her towards him.

'You come here,' he said, and she snuggled into him, the warmth and closeness of her short-circuiting his senses.

'I can do that,' she whispered, and he felt the silk of her hair brush against his chest, his cheek and tickle his nose. He pulled her closer.

He could do this. He could really do this. She fitted against him, he thought, she felt right. Yet, even as that thought formed, other darker ones chased it. Memories.

Never trust a woman, Ammar. Never let one close. Never show weakness.

He heard the angry echo of his father's voice, the cruel laughter of the woman he'd thought, naively, he'd loved. Felt the crack of his father's palm against his cheek, the rush of humiliation and shame dousing all desire.

Noelle brushed his cheek with her fingers, the touch as gentle as a whisper, and in surprise he opened his eyes, drawn from the agony of the past. 'Don't,' she said softly. 'Whatever it is, don't.' He gazed down at her, blinking in the darkness. He could barely make out her face, but he knew she looked completely serious.

'Don't what?'

'Don't let it control you,' Noelle said quietly. 'Don't let it win.'

Ammar drew her closer to him. 'I'm trying,' he said and yet, even then, with her in his arms, he wondered if it would be enough.

He must have slept, although it seemed to take an age. He heard Noelle's breathing finally deepen and slow in sleep and he remained holding her, in a sort of exquisite tension, enjoying the feel of her even as part of him longed for escape. Distance. Safety. And then, amazingly, sunlight streamed across the bed and it was morning, and he was slowly, languorously moving towards wakefulness, conscious only of the warm, round form fitted so closely to him, the flare of desire he felt in his groin as he moved his hand across her pliant softness, the silky fullness of a breast filling his hand.

Desire flared deeper and he rolled on top of her, his hands seeking her most private places as his lips moved over skin. He heard a moan and didn't know whether it came from him or her; it didn't matter. His hands slid over sleep-warmed skin, and her arms twined around him as he nudged apart her thighs with his knee.

'Ammar...'

Consciousness crashed over him and he froze, even as Noelle said his name again, reminding him who she was. Who he was. He would not make love to her like this, a hurried, desperate fumble, even if he wanted it so badly his body shook. Even if it would be easier to keep his mind blank, always blank, and just lose himself in her as quickly as he could.

No. She deserved more than that. Damn it, so did he. Slowly he rolled off her, flung one arm up over his head. His body shuddered with the loss of her, desire still pulsing through him, an undeniable ache.

'Ammar,' she said softly, and he heard all the hurt and rejection in her voice.

He knew he should explain. Apologise. *Say something.* But he just lay there, silent, his mind a numb, frozen wasteland. It took all of his effort, all his willpower to block out the memories.

Did you think I actually loved you, you stupid, foolish boy?

'Ammar, tell me what you're thinking.'

He dropped his arm, forced himself to meet her unhappy gaze. She nibbled her lip, her eyes swamped with uncertainty, dark with pain. 'I'm not thinking anything,' he said, and heard how remote he sounded. How cold. Why couldn't he gather her in his arms, explain to her that he wanted to make love to her, but he wanted to do it properly, without the fear of the memories swarming him, destroying him? He wanted to reassure her, but he was afraid of her rejection. Her revulsion. The words thickened in his throat, lodged in his chest like a stone. He stayed silent.

'I'm going to shower,' Noelle said and slipped out of bed and across the room. She was gone before Ammar could answer back.

Noelle walked quickly down the corridor to her own room, her head lowered, her vision near-blinded with tears. Stupid, to be crying *again.* Yet, no matter what Ammar said about desiring her or how beautiful she was, she still felt completely rejected, ugly and unloved when he rolled away from her, refused to make love to her as her body— and heart—demanded.

Why? Why had he turned away from her again? How could she believe he desired her when everything he did said he didn't? Miserably she turned on the shower as hot as she could stand it and, shrugging out of her nightie, stepped under the spray.

It had felt so good, so *right* to sleep in Ammar's arms last night…even if it had taken him an age to relax just a little bit, and even longer actually to fall asleep. Noelle had lain there, savouring the warmth and solid strength of him even as she longed for more. Always, she thought now, despair sweeping through her, longing for more.

And yet this morning, when he'd drawn her from sleep with his touch, every caress sending her spinning into pleasure…it had been wonderful. So sweet and yet so powerful, which made the crash to reality—and rejection once again—so much harder to bear.

Even now, doubt worked its corrosive power on her heart, her hope. How could Ammar care about her if he couldn't bear to touch her? How could he want a marriage when closeness of any kind was so painful for him?

How could any of this possibly *work?*

Resolutely Noelle turned off the shower and stepped out into the cool morning air. One day at a time, one *minute* at a time, if necessary. That was all either of them could take.

And yet doubt still whispered its treacherous message: *what if it doesn't work? What if he breaks your heart... again?*

Ammar turned to see Noelle coming down the stairs, her hair damp and pulled back into a loose ponytail. She looked pretty and fresh and so very lovely, but there were shadows in her eyes. Always the shadows. That morning, he knew, would cast a long one over the rest of the day. He would have to work hard to dispel it.

'I've had my housekeeper pack us a picnic,' he told her, managing a smile. 'And I've taken the liberty of packing you a few extra clothes—I don't think the clothes in your room ran to the sort of protective gear you need for desert travel.'

Noelle smiled back, although he felt that it took as much effort as his did. 'You know better than me,' she said.

Ammar led her out of the house to the soft-topped Jeep he'd driven round to the front of the property. Noelle slowed, gazing around at the sweep of desert, endless in every direction.

'So who sold you this piece of real estate?' she asked, and Ammar let out a rather rusty laugh.

'He told me there were ocean views from the top floor.'

Now she laughed, just a little bubble of sound that still made Ammar's heart sing. And reminded him that he still had a heart. 'I guess you were disappointed.'

'There is a small oasis about forty kilometres from here,' he told her as he started up the Jeep and headed away from the villa. There were no real roads, just old Bedouin tracks in the sand. It would be a bumpy ride.

'Seriously, though,' Noelle said. 'Why the desert? Why not a private island in the Med like your father?'

Ammar felt his hands tense around the steering wheel. 'I've been like my father in too many ways,' he said after a moment, his tone, he knew, cold and steely. He felt Noelle stiffen. She didn't want to hear about that. God knew, he didn't want to talk about it. Yet it remained between them, a heavy, palpable thing. At some point words would have to be said. Secrets confessed, shame admitted. 'In any case,' he added lightly, 'I've never liked Alhaja Island. I chose to live in the desert because it's the exact opposite. Space, freedom.'

'A sea of sand,' Noelle observed. 'You can still feel trapped.'

He glanced across at her and saw she was looking out at the sand, endless undulating waves of beige, punctuated only by occasional boulders, their edges sharp and unforgiving against the soft sweep of sand. 'Do you feel trapped?' he asked quietly.

She didn't answer for a long moment. Ammar's hands gripped the wheel so hard his joints ached. 'Let's talk about something else,' she finally said, still staring out at the sand, which Ammar knew was no answer at all.

Do you feel trapped?

How could she answer that? Yes, she did feel trapped, but not by the desert that stretched all around them. She felt trapped by memories, imprisoned by ignorance. She felt as if both she and Ammar were defined by their past hurts, and she didn't even know what his were. She struggled against her own fear of rejection, but it was hard. Too hard. How did you fight against that? How did you stop feeling trapped by what you felt, who you were?

'Where are we going?' she asked, knowing she needed to break out of the desperate circle of her thoughts. 'What is there to see in the Sahara?'

'I thought we could drive to that oasis I told you about. There are some interesting ruins there, the remains of a medieval trading post that were buried in a sandstorm hundreds of years ago. They were excavated by archaeologists a while back, but no one visits them much any more.'

'Well, it is quite a trip,' Noelle said lightly. 'How far away are we from the nearest city?'

'Marrakech is closest, about two hundred kilometres.'

'I suppose you value your privacy.'

'I do. I don't come here very often, though. I'm usually travelling for work.'

'And now you're the one in charge,' Noelle said, still trying to keep her tone light, although she knew they were venturing into deeper and dangerous waters. 'What will you do with Tannous Enterprises?'

'Legitimise it,' Ammar said flatly, and Noelle felt her heart squeeze at the admission, and the steely determination of his tone.

'What does that really mean?'

Ammar just shook his head. Noelle glanced at him, saw how his eyes were narrowed, although whether from the glare of the sun or some dark emotion she couldn't say.

'All right, let's talk about something else,' she said. 'What's your favourite colour?'

'What?' Startled, he glanced at her.

'Your favourite colour. Mine's green, although when I was little it was bubblegum-pink, pretty predictable, I know. I always wanted a dress in that colour, a Cinderella kind of dress.' She smiled as she turned to face him, keeping everything deliberately light. 'So what's yours?'

Ammar tilted his head, clearly giving the question some serious thought. It reminded Noelle, poignantly, of how he used to be when they'd dated, so intent and yet so gentle. *When I was with you, I was the man I wanted to be.* 'I don't,' Ammar finally said, 'have a favourite colour.'

'You must.'

'I must?' He glanced at her again, bemused. 'Why must I?'

'Everyone has a favourite colour.'

'I don't.'

She let out a laugh, half-exasperation, half-amusement. 'You decorated your dining room in red. You wouldn't have chosen that colour if you didn't like it—'

'I didn't choose it. I had someone decorate it for me.'

Of course. She couldn't quite see Ammar looking at paint samples. And yet he'd chosen her clothes. 'You told me you liked bright colours—'

'On you.'

'So perhaps a bright colour is your favourite,' Noelle suggested helpfully. 'Orange? Baby-blue? Or pink, like me?'

His lips twitched. 'None of the above.'

She sat back in her seat, arms folded. 'All right, I'll choose a colour for you.'

He arched his eyebrows, a tiny smile hovering now about his mouth. She loved his smiles, even the small ones. Each felt like a victory, a blessing. 'And what colour will you choose?'

Noelle considered. 'Yellow,' she finally said. It was the

colour of sunshine and mornings and freshness. The colour of hope. And she needed some hope.

'Yellow,' Ammar repeated and she nodded.

'Yes. Yellow.'

'Well, there's plenty of yellow in the desert,' he said
after a moment. 'So perhaps it is my favourite colour after
all.'

'Maybe that's why you chose to live here,' Noelle said,
a teasing lilt entering her voice. 'Even without the ocean
view.'

The corner of his mouth quirked upwards. 'Even without.' Then he shook his head slowly, a frown drawing his
brows together. 'But the realtor *promised* ocean views.'

She let out a sudden burst of laughter. 'For a second
there, I almost believed you.'

'I know I don't joke very often.'

'I like it,' Noelle said quietly. 'I like when you smile,
and especially when you laugh.'

His glance flicked to her, his smile softening his features, every trace of harshness gone. 'You always brought
that out in me.'

'I did?'

'From the moment I met you. You made me laugh, even
when I had nothing to laugh about.'

Noelle's heart seemed to turn right over. Silently she
reached for his hand and Ammar laced his fingers through
hers. Neither of them spoke, but they didn't need to. The
silence was a golden thread drawing and binding them
together.

Eventually Noelle leaned her head against the seat and
closed her eyes. Sitting there with the sun on her face and
the breeze blowing over her, she felt an easing inside, an
unfurling and blossoming of a long-dormant seed, a seed
of happiness. Of hope.

'We're here.'

She must have dozed, for Ammar nudged her gently and she realised she was leaning against his shoulder. She felt the heat of him, inhaled the tangy, spicy scent of his aftershave and scrambled to a seated position.

'Sorry. I was lulled to sleep by the Jeep, I suppose.'

'More like jolted to sleep,' Ammar said with a little smile. Three smiles today, Noelle thought, and counting. 'Let's take a look around.'

The oasis was still and lovely, a placid little sea of blue fringed by palms, flung down in the desert by an almighty hand. Noelle bent down to trail her fingers through the warm water.

'There aren't any creatures in here, are there?' she asked a bit belatedly.

'Just a snake or two, but they tend to be shy.'

She jerked her hand back before she realised he was teasing her. 'You're actually joking,' she said. 'Again.'

He raised his eyebrows. 'Must be a good day.'

'A very good day,' she agreed. She straightened, smiling. 'You did find my *toc-toc* joke funny, back in the day.'

'S-cargot.'

A thrill ran through her, that he'd remembered. 'It was pretty dreadful, I know.'

'No, no, it was good.' He smiled—that made four now, and this was a proper one—his hands in his pockets as he tilted his face up to the sun. 'Very good. I don't like to eat them, though.'

'Eat them?' Noelle repeated rather dazedly, for the sight of Ammar's smile had plunged her into a sudden spinning void of lust. He was an unbearably attractive man, even with the buzz-cut and the scar. She would never grow tired of looking at him, of gazing at the hard angles of his cheek and jaw, the sexy, sculpted pout of his lips, the lean, powerful lines of his chest and shoulders. And, more than that, she would never tire of the way his eyes lightened to bronze when he smiled, and how that single, simple curving of his lips made her feel as if she'd scaled Everest, as if she were on top of the world.

Ammar turned and caught her looking at him and Noelle knew every emotion was reflected in her eyes, visible on her face. 'Snails,' he clarified huskily, and Noelle scrambled to make sense of what he was saying, which was exceedingly difficult when all she could think about was how wonderful he looked and how much she wanted to touch him.

'Snails,' she repeated, still dazed, still filled with desire. Ammar reached for her hand. His own face was inscrutable as always, yet his eyes blazed intent. Or was she just hoping they did, and that he felt the same tidal wave of lust that was crashing over her? He'd felt it last night, she knew he had, and this morning, too—he'd wanted her. She had to believe that. She just didn't know why he'd stopped.

'Come on,' he said. 'I'll show you the ruins.'

She let him take her hand and lead her to the ruins a little way from the water. At first the remnants of the medieval city looked like no more than boulders scattered in the sand but, as Ammar led her through, pointed out the foundations of a house, the still straight line of a road, she saw the order of it, a civilization lost for centuries.

'What happened?' she asked, turning in a circle as she stood in what Ammar had said was most likely a shop. He braced one hip against a weathered piece of wall, his eyes narrowed against the sun's glare.

'No one knows for certain, but archaeologists believe a sandstorm covered the entire town about six hundred years ago. Destroyed everything in a single day.'

'Wow.' Noelle swallowed and studied the remnants of

that day. *I know what that feels like.* She didn't say it, didn't even want to think it. For once she didn't want the pain of the past to interfere with the present. The sun was shining, Ammar was smiling and the day stretched before them, promising, maybe even perfect. 'Show me the rest,' she said, and he reached for her hand again.

They wandered through the rest of the ruins hand in hand, stopping to pace out a house or examine a doorstep or window well. It was amazingly relaxed, natural even, in a way that made Noelle's heart sing. She wanted this day to go on for ever.

Eventually Ammar led her back towards the oasis, to a sheltered spot where a couple of palm trees shaded them from the relentless sun. She watched as he spread out a blanket, desire spiralling inside her once again as she gazed at his lean brown arms, powerfully corded with muscle, the T-shirt he wore clinging to his washboard stomach. She sucked in a breath as he glanced up at her, his amber eyes seeming to burn into her. He must know how he affected her, she thought. He *must*. She only hoped she affected him the same way.

'Come here,' he commanded huskily and, with a thrill of both nervousness and hope, Noelle went to him. He took her by the hand and tugged her down to the blanket, his knee nudging hers, his body so very close.

'Shall we eat?' he said, and his voice sounded hoarse. *He feels it,* Noelle thought, *he must feel it.*

'OK.' Her voice was a scratchy whisper. She struggled to eat, even though each morsel he gave her was delicious. Her hand shook as she finally accepted a fig from him, soft and ripe. *Touch me,* she wanted to cry. *Touch me. Show me you love me.* She bit into the fig, its lush sweetness filling her mouth, yet she was only conscious of Ammar watching her, his gaze so heavy and intent.

Her whole body felt hot, liquid, the centre of her starting to melt. She felt a bit of juice from the fig dribble down her chin and Ammar reached forward and swiped at it with his thumb. Her lips parted, her eyes closed, her body instinctively giving every signal it could to show him how much she desired him.

With a groan of surrender—or was it despair?—Ammar cupped her face with both of his hands and drew her to him. The feel of his lips on hers was like a drink of water in the desert, as life-giving as the oasis itself. She *needed* him.

She brought her hands up to his shoulders, pulled him closer, pressing herself against him as her head fell back in helpless assent. She didn't speak, terrified to break the moment, the spell of desire that had surely been cast over both of them, for Ammar was kissing her hungrily, his tongue delving into the softness of her mouth, his hands finding the fullness of her breasts.

He stretched out beside her, sliding his hand under her shirt, his touch warm and sure. It felt so unbelievably, unbearably good, and Noelle could not keep herself from pressing his hand against her tummy, holding it there, because she was still so afraid he would stop.

He lifted her shirt higher and bent his head to her breasts, nudging the lace of her bra aside. Noelle heard a sound come from her own mouth, a moan of intense longing she'd never heard herself make before. 'Oh, Ammar,' she whispered. She swallowed down the words she wanted to say. *I love you.* 'I want you so much.'

She felt him still, tense. *Oh, no, please,* she thought, *please don't pull away from me again.* What was *wrong* with her?

The moment seemed suspended, endless. His lips still

brushed her breast, his hands on her skin. Neither of them moved or spoke. Noelle didn't even breathe.

Please...

Then, deliberately, as if it were a decision he had to make, Ammar lifted his head and kissed her on the mouth, deeply, a promise. Relief and need poured through her, an overwhelming rush of emotion. She reached for him instinctively, her hand skimming along his chest and torso, pulling her to him, but suddenly Ammar tensed and rolled away and Noelle let out a cry of frustration and, far worse, hurt.

'Why do you do that?' She sat up, stared at him, still lying on the ground, his body rigid, his arm flung over his face just as before. 'I know you want me. Physically, at least—'

'It's not you.' He spoke flatly, his face still covered. 'It's never been about you.'

'Really? Because it feels like it's about me. I'm the one you push away, the person you reject—' She heard how sharp her voice sounded, but that was better than letting him see how devastated she felt. She struggled to sit up, pulling her shirt down to cover herself.

Ammar didn't say anything. He was staring up at the sky as if he were cloud-gazing on a perfect summer's day, as if nothing were remotely wrong.

Fury rose up inside her, clawed its way out. 'Don't *do* that. Don't blank me out. I hate it when you do that.' Her voice shook and in a sudden burst of frustration she reached over and hit him hard on the shoulder.

He caught her hand in one quick movement, held it, firmly yet with leashed strength, in his. 'Don't hit me,' he said in a cold, flat voice she barely recognised. 'Don't ever hit me.'

Noelle stared at him, her hand still caught in his, his

face so blank and remote, everything about him distant and *strange,* and with a choked cry she yanked her hand away and struggled up from the blanket. Ammar still said nothing, didn't react at all, and blindly she turned and strode away from him, through the long grass.

CHAPTER SEVEN

DAMN. He'd handled that completely wrong. He'd acted on instinct, which was just about the worst thing he could have done. When it came to Noelle, Ammar knew, he needed to act *against* his instincts. And in moments like the one they'd just shared, that felt near impossible.

He heard the whisper of the grass fringing the water and knew she was walking around the oasis. He hoped she had the sense not to stray into the desert. He should follow her, say something. But what? He had no words. Nothing inside him. Yet he knew he couldn't stay blank for ever, even if part of him longed to.

It would be easier, he thought, and simpler, just to let her go. Set her free, just as he'd done before. If he were stronger, he would do it. But he wasn't, and he needed her too much. Even if she didn't think he did.

And as for what Noelle felt… The very fact that she'd stayed, that she'd wanted to stay, meant something. She might not love or trust him yet—and God only knew why she should—but something in her called out to him, from the first moment they'd met. They had brought out the best in each other, even if they were seeing the worst now.

When I was with you, I was the man I wanted to be.

He'd spoken from the heart when he'd told her that, meant it utterly. Those few months in London were the happiest of his life. He'd been twenty-seven years old and most of his life had been a barren, loveless landscape, like living on the moon. Cold and lifeless…until Noelle. Until she'd woken him up, gave him glimpses of the kind of life he'd never dreamed he could have. And he'd lived in that dream for two months, not thinking of the future or reality at all until his wedding day, when his father had woken him up with the cold, hard truth.

She's just a woman, Ammar. You will show your wife her place. And if you don't, I will.

He'd been furious, powerless and completely trapped. The only thing he'd felt he could do was walk away from her.

And it was easier for you, wasn't it, keeping your secrets? She never had to know the truth of who you are. What you've done, what you're capable of.

Ammar closed his eyes, the recriminations pouring through him, a scalding river of regret. The past tormented him even as he ached to forget it, to forge a future where he was different. Where he was with Noelle.

When I was with you, I was the man I wanted to be.

He needed to be that man now.

Slowly, his body aching, he rose from the blanket. He walked around the oasis, the sun beating down so the tranquil surface shimmered like a metal plate. The air was still and drowsy with the heat of mid-afternoon; nothing moved. Halfway round he saw her, sitting on a flat rock that jutted out towards the water. She sat with her arms wrapped around her knees, her chin resting on top, her hair tumbling about her shoulders and hiding her face. She looked, he thought, as lovely as ever, and completely miserable.

He stopped a few feet away, but she didn't move, didn't

even look at him. He had no idea what to say. Life had not prepared him for moments like this.

'I'm sorry,' he finally said. It seemed as good a place to start as any. He *was* sorry.

She glanced at him, her expression guarded. 'What are you sorry for?'

Was this a trick question? Ammar hesitated. He was sorry for so many things. Sorry for walking away from her all those years ago, without even explaining why. Sorry he'd had to walk away, that he'd felt trapped and hopeless. And sorry—desperately, painfully sorry—that his past still tormented them both now, that he was afraid he would never be free of it. 'I'm sorry,' he said, 'for hurting you.'

Her face hardened, and so did her voice. 'How did you hurt me, Ammar?'

He felt the first familiar flicker of anger. What was this—a test? Clearly there was a right answer and he had no idea what it was. 'Why don't you tell me how I hurt you,' he asked evenly.

She raised her eyebrows. 'Turning the question back to me? How very neat.'

He felt himself grit his teeth and forced his jaw to relax. 'I don't want to fight.'

She let out a shuddering sigh and shook her head, her hair tumbling about her shoulders once more. The sunlight caught gleaming strands of gold and amber amid the deep chestnut brown. 'I don't want to fight, either,' she said quietly. 'But I can't...' She trailed off, biting her lip, and Ammar felt everything in him freeze.

'Can't what?'

She just shook her head and looked away, and Ammar thought, *I'm losing her. I'm not sure I ever really had her, but what I might have had I'm losing now.*

He felt as if he couldn't breathe, as if he were suffocating in his own silence. He didn't know what to say. What words she needed to hear.

The truth.

The answer was so simple, so blindingly obvious, and so awful. He didn't want to tell her the truth. He couldn't stand being so vulnerable, so utterly exposed, and having her look at him in hatred or pity or even revulsion—

She let out a soft, sorrowful sigh and rose from the rock. 'Let's go back,' she said without looking at him and Ammar clenched his fists.

'Wait.'

She stopped, looked at him over her shoulder, her eyes dark and wide. Waiting, just as he'd asked. Ammar took a deep breath. He closed his eyes, summoned what strength he could. 'I can't,' he said, and she stared.

'Can't what?'

The same question he'd asked her, and she hadn't answered. Neither could he. He felt as if his soul were being scraped raw, his skin peeled away. He *hated* this. 'I want you, you know that, physically, but…when we…something happens…' He stopped, a vein beating in his temple, a familiar fury longing to cloak him with its protection. *No.* Anger was a cover-up for fear. He had to see this through.

Her eyes widened, her mouth parting softly. 'What…' She moistened her lips with the tip of her tongue. 'What are you saying?'

Where to begin? He stared at her, the softness of her hair and the fullness of her lips, the perfect creamy *innocence* of her, and he had no idea what to say. How to start. 'My life has been very different from yours,' he said flatly, and her gaze flew to his, clearly startled.

'Tell me,' she said quietly, and he let out a shuddering breath. No excuses now, even if talking about this was the worst form of torture. It brought every memory and fear to the fore, made him feel afresh the raw humiliation and helpless anger he'd felt before, as a boy. He sure as hell didn't want to feel that with Noelle.

'Ammar,' she said, and his name sounded, strangely, like an affirmation, an encouragement. He could do this. With her, he could do this.

'I told you about my father. How he had…very definite ideas about what a son, a man, should be.' She nodded, alert and listening. 'Everything was a lesson with him, a way to learn.' He saw her frown, just faintly, and knew she didn't really understand. How could she? He knew he could give her details, examples—horrible, painful examples—but he didn't want to tell her about how his father had broken every belief about love he'd ever had, broken *him*. He didn't want to gain her pity along with her understanding. He couldn't bear that. No, he'd just cut to the relevant part. The part about Leila.

'There was a maid in my father's house,' he began, 'on Alhaja. She was very pretty, but more than that, she…she seemed kind. When…' his throat closed up and he swallowed hard '…when things had been particularly difficult for me, she always offered a kind word. Listened to me, not that I ever said much. I suppose I saw her as a friend at first, but more than that.' Even now he remembered how he'd talked to her, clumsily, honestly, baring his heart in a way he hadn't since…even if he'd wanted to. Even if Noelle had made him want to. 'I suppose,' he said, his voice so low he wasn't even sure if Noelle could hear him, 'I began to think I loved her.'

Noelle said nothing. She looked pale, her eyes wide, her lips pressed together. 'What happened?' she finally asked, and Ammar realised he had stopped speaking.

'She seduced me. I was fourteen years old; I'd never even touched a woman that way. And my father…my father had paid her to do it all—the kindness, the smiles and, of course, the seduction. And then—' He stopped, hating that he had to tell this part of the sordid tale. 'When we… when we were going to…she rejected me. Told me she was only pretending to be interested in me because my father had paid her to teach me a lesson.'

Noelle drew back. 'A *lesson*?'

'Everything was a lesson with him,' Ammar said flatly. 'A means to an end, a way to mould me into the shape he deemed fit.'

'And what lesson,' she asked after a moment, her voice shaking, 'was that maid?'

'Never trust a woman, or become close to her. Never show weakness.' He recited the mantras in a monotone; he could almost hear his father's harsh voice repeating the words.

'That's terrible,' Noelle said quietly. Ammar said nothing. He agreed with her, but what difference did it make? What difference did telling her make, if he couldn't change after all? 'And so,' she continued slowly, 'that's what this is about? You don't trust me?'

'I haven't trusted anyone,' Ammar said. 'I haven't let anyone close, except for you.' And every time he tried to be close with her, as physically close as he so desperately wanted to be, his mind froze and the memories took over. So he went blank, just as he'd done as a boy, a child, because that was what he did. That was how he survived. It was simple, really. Basic psychology. Yet understanding what he did—and why—didn't make it any easier to stop. No matter how much he wanted to.

Noelle was silent for a long moment, her head bowed, her hair covering her face. He wished he could see her expression, her eyes. 'Do I remind you of that maid?' she asked finally, and he heard the hurt in her voice. 'Do I look like her or something?'

Ammar sighed, the sound one of both resignation and impatience. 'Not at all. I've never...' He hesitated, his hands instinctively curling into fists. Noelle looked up, waiting. 'I've never felt about anyone what I feel for you.'

'Even that maid?'

'Even her.'

She was silent for a long moment. 'And on our wedding night?' she finally asked. 'And in the hotel two months later? Were you...did you feel this way then?'

Ammar let out a shuddering breath. 'Yes—'

'So you didn't just mean to let me go?' She sounded sad, but he heard the accusation.

'It was complicated,' he said tightly.

'Oh, Ammar—'

'No more questions,' he snapped, and she blinked, looked down. *Damn.* He wasn't handling this right but, God help him, how was he supposed to handle it? He felt as if he had just shed every defence, every protection, and it was horrible, all the old scabbed wounds were being ripped open, raw and bleeding. He had to fight the urge to either attack or retreat, not just stand here and take it. Listen to her questions and even answer them. 'We've talked about this enough.'

'Have we?'

Impatience bit at him. 'Noelle, I've told you more about my past, about myself, than I have to another living soul. And every word is like a drop of blood.' He forced himself to speak calmly. 'Could we just take a break from this conversation? For a little while?' She said nothing and he let out a long, slow breath. 'Please.'

She gazed at him, her eyes dark and wide. 'Yes,' she said softly. 'Of course we can.' And relief so deep poured through him that he felt as if his body shook from it. He drew a shuddering breath, managed a smile. 'We should head back home. I'd rather drive in the daylight.'

'OK.' She slid off the rock and, to Ammar's shock, she reached for his hand. His fingers curled around hers as a matter of both instinct and need. 'Let's go,' she said, and she led the way back to the Jeep.

Noelle walked hand in hand with Ammar, her mind spinning with what he'd just told her. It must have cost him to confess such secrets to her. It must have cost him so much.

They walked silently through the long grass and in her mind's eye she saw Ammar as she remembered him from her own childhood, a sullen, lanky boy with liquid eyes and a reluctant, beautiful smile. What kind of childhood had he had with a father like that? What kind of *life* had he had?

The thought of her own father teaching her such a cruel and malicious lesson was unthinkable. Yet Ammar had learned such lessons, it would seem, over and over again. No wonder honest, loving intimacy of any kind was so difficult for him.

She thought of the door knob turning on her wedding night. Ammar flinging her away from him when she'd reached for him that awful evening in the hotel. Kissing her the other night, rolling away from her today. He desired her; she'd felt it, known it. And now she believed it, understood he'd never really been rejecting her. He'd just been fighting his own demons. His memories. And now he'd finally shared them with her, shared the most intimate and revealing thing about himself. For a man intent on being invulnerable it was a pretty amazing thing to do. It was a miracle.

Ammar opened the passenger door of the Jeep and

helped her inside. She could feel the tension in his body, saw a muscle flickering in his jaw. She knew he hated her knowing his secrets, hated feeling so exposed.

She laid a hand on his arm, felt the muscles jerk under her touch and then he stilled, his face half-averted.

'Thank you,' she said quietly, 'for telling me.'

He didn't speak, just nodded, his face still turned from hers. It would have to be enough.

They didn't speak on the way home and when they got back to the house Ammar excused himself with work. Noelle wandered up to her bedroom, restless, her mind still spinning.

She spent the afternoon lying on her bed, watching the shadows lengthen on the floor, her mind in a daze as memories paraded through her consciousness, a montage of remembrances that were made even more poignant and bittersweet by this new knowledge.

She saw it all differently now, from Ammar's perspective. She saw a man who longed for love, yet whose life had forced him to spurn it on every level: physical, emotional, spiritual. And yet still he'd wanted and, more than that, he'd *tried*. It made her, she realised, love him more.

And she revelled in the freedom of knowing, all those years ago, and even last night, that it hadn't been her. He hadn't been rejecting her, not the way she'd always feared. She believed him completely now, knew he did find her desirable. And that knowledge was both thrilling and wonderful.

She felt as if the fear that had dogged and haunted her for so many years had finally fallen away. She was free— free to love Ammar as she knew now she wanted to, love him fully and deeply and completely.

And she wanted to tell him so.

She watched the room darken and twilight settle on

the rolling desert hills, casting long violet shadows on the sand. She felt a new sense of both peace and purpose, and with a smile she swung her legs off the bed and went in search of Ammar.

He wasn't anywhere in the house and so she went out into the garden, now cloaked in darkness. She heard the sound of water slapping the sides of the pool and stopped a little distance away, watched as Ammar cut smoothly and assuredly through the water. He was a good swimmer; perhaps that, in part, had saved his life. She watched him for a moment more before an idea came to her. Smiling a little, even as her heart began to thud with frantic, fearful beats, she turned around and went back to her room.

Ammar swam with sure, even strokes, the movement propelling him forward, taking over his thoughts. Exercise was, he had long ago discovered, a great way to work off anger and blank his mind out at the same time. Just what he'd needed when his father had made one of his repellent requests. Call in a loan. Demand a bribe. Lie, cheat, steal. Over the years he'd stopped thinking about what he was doing, refused to remember the conscience that had pricked him as a still-naïve boy.

But, Papa—

The only answer had been his father's fist.

Ammar increased his speed. He could feel his heart thudding in his chest. He didn't want to think. Couldn't remember. Not his father, not all the things he'd done, and most certainly not the look on Noelle's face when he'd told her about his past. His weakness.

He finished another lap and hauled himself onto the side of the pool, his heart beating so hard it hurt. His lungs ached and water ran down his face and chest in rivulets.

He drew in a shuddering breath and was resolutely turning back to the pool when he heard her.

'There you are.'

He turned, surprise streaking through him like lightning at the sight of her. Noelle stood in front of him, dressed only in a forest-green string bikini. He'd bought the bikini so it shouldn't surprise him to see her wearing it. He'd *wanted* to see her wearing it, had imagined peeling it slowly from her body. Now he saw it fitted at least, unlike the other clothes. It fitted very well.

She smiled and sat on the edge of the pool, sliding her long, shapely legs into the water. She had the most gorgeous skin, Ammar thought, like golden cream. The top two triangles of the bikini left very little to the imagination and he found his gaze was riveted by the sight of her really rather perfect breasts barely covered by those scraps of cloth. Bikinis, he thought, were indecent. Indecently beautiful.

'The water's warm,' she said, trailing her fingers through it. She had to lean over to do it, giving him an even better glimpse of her breasts. Ammar felt himself harden. He wanted her now, had always wanted her, imagined pulling her into the pool and taking her right there. Didn't they both need the release?

And yet he knew what would happen if he did just that. The memories would take him over, shrieking inside his head, and his mind would go blank—the only way he knew of dealing with it—and he'd push her away. And now she knew why. She knew his most pathetic, shaming secret and he hated it. Why the hell was she here?

'I was just getting out,' he said, knowing he sounded surly.

'Don't go just when I got here,' she protested with a playful smile, but he just shook his head.

'I have work to do.'

'At night?'

'I have many responsibilities, Noelle.' He sounded like a schoolteacher.

'Am I one of them?' She arched her eyebrows, her legs stretched out, and with one toe she gave him a little splash. She was flirting, he realised in disbelief, or trying to. It reminded him of how she used to be, light and smiling and playful, and how he'd been with her. Trying to unbend. Learning to love.

'I'm busy,' he snapped, and he saw her smile falter. She glanced downwards, biting her lip, and he felt like the biggest jerk in the world. 'I'm sorry,' he said grudgingly.

She glanced back up at him, her playful smile resolutely restored. 'So you'll stay?'

And, unbelievably, he found himself nodding. 'All right. Fine.' He'd stay, but he'd still sound like an ass.

Reluctantly Ammar watched her. She'd leaned over the pool again, gazing into the water, and if she leaned out much more she was going to pop right out of that bikini.

'You're too thin,' he said abruptly, and Noelle glanced at him in surprise.

'You're being unusually charming tonight, Ammar.'

'You are,' he insisted. He knew he was saying all the wrong things but the right ones terrified him too much. And he was pretty sure he didn't want to hear what she might have to say. 'Why have you lost so much weight?'

Noelle shrugged. 'I work in the fashion industry. You've got to be thin.'

'I liked you better before. You were softer then.'

Her eyes flashed sudden fire. 'Funny, but I could say the same thing about you.'

He let out a surprised, rusty laugh. She smiled and for a moment he felt lighter. For a moment he could let himself just *be*, enjoying the sight of a beautiful woman in a bikini. A woman he loved.

Terror clutched at him again and she shook her head. 'Stop thinking so much, Ammar.'

'What are you talking about?'

'I can see it in your eyes. You start to look like a trapped rabbit—'

'Are you,' he growled, 'comparing me to a *rabbit*?'

'Yes.' Her smile deepened, her eyes gleaming. 'At least your eyes.' Her gaze wandered slowly, deliberately over his bare chest and then lower. 'Not the rest of you.'

His body responded to her obviously appreciative gaze. She slid off the side of the pool and waded towards him. When she was just a handspan away—so close he could inhale the sweet fragrance that he knew didn't come from any soap or perfume but was just *her*—she lifted her hand and trailed one fingertip down the length of his chest, leaving goose bumps in its wake.

Ammar froze. Now he felt trapped, as trapped as a damned rabbit, caught between desire and that old instinctive fear. She was so close and he wanted her closer, even as he craved that distance and safety.

'I want to help you,' she said, and she might as well have poured ice cubes down his back. Into his heart.

'I don't want your *help*,' he snapped, and she fell silent.

'Help was the wrong word,' she said quietly. 'I want to love you, Ammar.'

She gazed up at him, expectant, hopeful, her eyes wide and clear, reflecting every emotion. Ammar said nothing. She bit her lip, taking its lush fullness between her teeth in a way that felt like a kick to the heart. He wanted to tell her he loved her, knew she needed to hear it, yet the words lodged in his chest, burning a hole in his heart.

I love you. Why couldn't he say it? Three silly little

words. Except there was nothing silly about them because he meant them utterly, with every fibre of his being. *I love you.* The last time he'd said those words, the woman on the receiving end had laughed in his face. Told him, the naked, naïve fourteen-year-old boy that he'd been, that she was only here on his father's orders. He'd been devastated, of course he had, but he should have got over it. Should have moved on like any normal man would.

When he'd fallen in love with Noelle, when he'd drawn her to him and felt the explosion of fear in his chest, he knew he hadn't. He'd thought it would be different when they married. He'd still so desperately wanted to believe he could have it all. Have her. Then his dreams had all come crashing down when his father had confronted him on what he'd hoped would be the happiest night of his life.

You will show your wife her place. And if you don't, I will. Why do you persist in these naïve schoolboy dreams?

He'd known then just how weak he was. Too weak to admit the truth to Noelle. Too weak to let her know of his fear, his shame, the kind of life he'd lived. Too weak to risk it—or to stand up to his father.

'Ammar.' Noelle placed her hands on either side of his face and reached up on tiptoe to brush her lips against his own. He didn't respond, felt everything inside him shut down, every response a big blank. What kind of man was he?

Hopeless.

'I don't think you realise,' she said softly, 'how much it means to me, that you told me—'

'Don't—' Numb as he was, he knew he couldn't stand her pity.

'That you were never rejecting me,' Noelle continued. She was smiling, although he could see tears shimmering in her eyes. She still held his face in her hands, his heart.

He couldn't move. 'That you never actually found me undesirable or ugly.'

He swallowed, his throat so tight it hurt to get the words out. 'You're the loveliest woman I've ever seen.'

A tear slid down her cheek. 'I believe you now,' she whispered. 'I believe you completely, and that's the most wonderful feeling in the world.'

'Is it?' His voice came out in a hoarse whisper. His throat ached. His body ached. Everything inside him hurting.

'You set me free, you know, with the truth. Free to love you without fear.'

He'd never thought of it that way. He had, he knew, only been thinking about his own shame and pain and weakness, and hiding it from her. Not what she might be feeling. What it might make her believe about herself. Carefully he brushed the tear still sliding down her cheek with his thumb. 'I'm sorry.'

She shook her head, another tear spilling down her cheek. He caught it with his other thumb, his hands now cupping her face, his palms sliding against the exquisite softness of her skin. 'Don't be sorry. Not about—'

'Don't.' *Don't pity me,* he almost said, but he couldn't bear to say the words.

'We can work through this, Ammar.'

He dropped his hands from her face, took a much-needed step away. 'I don't want to *work through* anything.'

She blinked. 'You don't want things to change?'

God, yes, he wanted everything to change. 'What I don't want,' he said shortly, 'is to have this conversation.'

'There seem to be a lot of conversations you don't want to have.' She cocked her head, studying him so he felt like some wretched specimen. 'You haven't been celibate your whole life,' she said slowly. 'That much I know. You've been with plenty of other women, I'd guess.'

'Enough,' he allowed.

'How?'

He said nothing. He wasn't about to tell her about the sordid, soulless encounters he'd had that passed for relationships in his sorry life.

'I suppose,' Noelle said after a moment, 'you've been able to separate it in your mind. Sex and emotion. Sex and love.' Still he didn't answer. 'I tried to do that, you know,' she said softly. 'After…after our annulment. I wanted to feel desired, and so I went searching for it in a bunch of empty relationships. Flings.'

Jealousy flared through him, burning white-hot. He hadn't expected her to have stayed a virgin for ten years, but it still hurt. He certainly hadn't been celibate, although the women he'd been with had never meant anything to him at all. He made sure they didn't, always kept it a mutually pleasurable and meaningless transaction. Mind firmly disengaged. Only Noelle had opened up the emotion and yearning inside him, and also the memories. The fear.

'All of it made me feel worse than before,' Noelle said quietly. 'Emptier than ever.'

He nodded tersely. He knew how that went. Both of them had been searching for the one thing they could only find in each other. And still didn't have. Frustration burst through him at the thought.

'I knew I wanted something more, but I was afraid to try for it.' She took a breath. 'The only man who has ever made me want to try is you.' She tilted her face up towards him, her expression so unbearably open and searching. He knew she was waiting. Waiting for those three words.

I love you.

He opened his mouth. Nothing came out. He saw disappointment flicker in her eyes and he took a step back. 'I should do some work.' A completely lame excuse, but he couldn't think of anything better.

Noelle didn't challenge him. She just nodded slowly, and Ammar wondered if that flicker of disappointment was already turning to defeat. Swallowing, he took another step away and then hauled himself out of the pool.

Noelle remained alone in the water, Ammar's silence echoing through her. She'd thought he was going to tell her he loved her, but of course it wasn't so easy or quick. Had she actually thought that she could solve everything in the space of an afternoon? She still was ridiculously naïve.

She let out a long, slow breath, unsure what to do now. She had a feeling Ammar needed some space and maybe she did, too. Glancing around at the tranquil pool, she decided she might as well swim.

Fifty laps later, she was exhausted and freezing; the sun had set and the desert night air was sharp with cold. At least she'd blanked her thoughts out for a little while. Not thinking had been its own relief, just like she supposed it was with Ammar. She hauled herself out of the pool, surprised to see a thick terry cloth robe lying on one of the deckchairs. She hadn't brought it, so someone else must have while she was swimming. Had Ammar? Or one of his staff who slipped through the house like ghosts, tidying and cleaning the only signs they'd been there at all?

She slipped it on, grateful for its warmth, and headed back towards the French windows that led into the music room. She came to a surprised halt as she rounded a bend in the path; a small table, flickering with candlelight and set for two, had been brought out into the private little garden. Ammar stood there, dressed in a white button-down shirt and dark grey trousers, looking incredible and so very sexy as he opened a bottle of wine.

'What—'

'I thought you might be hungry.' He looked tense, but still he gave a small smile as he poured two glasses.

'I am,' Noelle admitted. She was touched, and thrilled really, that Ammar had thought to provide such a romantic setting for their meal. She'd been bracing herself for another tense confrontation, and it meant so much that he'd chosen this instead. 'It looks wonderful,' she said. 'I just need to get dressed.'

'I'll be waiting.'

She practically flew upstairs, stripping off the robe and bikini and searching through the racks of clothes Ammar had bought for something suitable to wear. She pulled on a white cotton blouse and pale green linen skirt; like the other clothes, they were too big but she didn't have much choice and she wanted to hurry. She was afraid if she took too long downstairs would disappear like a mirage; Ammar would blow out the candles and retreat back into his cold, autocratic self. Grabbing a brush, she decided she'd tackle the wet tangle of her hair later.

As she stepped through the French windows she saw, with a dizzying wave of relief, that it was all the same. The wine, the candlelight, Ammar. The candlelight flickered over his face, the lean planes of his jaw and cheek, the scar lost in shadow. He'd left the top two buttons of his shirt open, and Noelle's gaze was helplessly drawn to the brown column of his throat, the sculpted lines of his chest so warm looking in the candlelight. She swallowed dryly, every thought flying from her head. How, she wondered dazedly, could you want someone so much?

Ammar turned and, although he remained still, she saw something flash in his eyes, turning them to gold. She held her breath, felt tension and desire snap through the air, and then he gestured to her hand. 'Let me,' he said, and belatedly Noelle realised she was still holding her hairbrush and her hair was in wet rats' tails about her face. Lovely. She must look a sight, breathless and unbrushed. She had no make-up on and her feet were bare.

'I hurried,' she muttered, and Ammar took the brush from her hand.

'I'm glad.'

He tugged on her hand and she let him lead her to one of the chairs. She closed her eyes as he worked the brush through her hair, his touch so tender and gentle it would have brought tears to her eyes if she wasn't already pulsing with desire.

'I've always loved your hair,' he said, his voice an ache. 'A thousand shades.' She felt his fingers on her neck, massaging the tense muscles, and she let out a breathy sigh of pleasure.

'Do you remember,' she asked, her eyes closed, the touch of his fingers so mesmerising that she had to fish for each word, forming them slowly, 'when you brushed my hair before?'

Ammar didn't answer for a moment, just kept brushing her hair with long, sensuous strokes, his touch deft and sure and gentle, each stroke of the hairbrush seeming to blaze down Noelle's back, igniting her with need, even as a wonderful languor flowed through her veins. 'I remember,' he finally said in a voice that throbbed with the memory of it.

Neither of them spoke, the moment seeming to spin on and on between them. She could hear each breath he drew, felt the heat of his body so close to hers. It felt incredibly intimate, even though she couldn't see him. It felt as if each stroke of the brush released the memories and fear they both had, the pain and hurt and shame, a tender act of both healing and hope.

'There,' he finally said and, setting the brush down he carefully moved her hair aside and pressed a kiss to the nape of her neck, just as he had once before. Noelle let out a shuddering breath as his lips lingered on her skin. 'I love you,' he said softly, and her heart expanded so it seemed to fill her whole chest. She couldn't breathe.

'I love you, too,' she whispered. 'So much.' She hadn't said that before, had only told him she *wanted* to love him. As if it was difficult. A challenge instead of a joy. Now she understood how simple it could be, how perfect and pure.

Silently, Ammar reached for her hand, threaded her fingers through his. She still couldn't see him, although she felt the solid strength of him behind her, his warm breath fanning her ear. And in that moment she felt her whole self buoy with happiness; she felt as if she could float right up to the sky, and no more so than when Ammar whispered, his voice rough with emotion and want, 'Come upstairs with me. Forget dinner and come upstairs with me right now.'

CHAPTER EIGHT

SILENTLY, Ammar led her to his bedroom, his fingers still threaded with hers. Noelle could feel her heart thudding in her chest, each painful beat reminding her of the intimacy and importance of this moment, of what Ammar was asking. Finally they would have their wedding night.

He opened the door to his bedroom and drew her inside. In the shadowy moonlit room she could only just make out his face, and saw how solemn and intent he looked. Her heart beat harder.

He let out a shuddering breath and to her dismay took a step back, releasing her hand. She felt the loss of him acutely, the emptiness like an ache. She held her breath, watching him warily as he drew another deep breath.

'I've waited so long for this,' he said in a low voice that throbbed with emotion. 'So long, and I'm not rushing it like some randy schoolboy.'

'I don't mind rushing,' Noelle said shakily and Ammar gave her a small smile.

'There will be time for rushing later. Now we're going to take it slowly.' And his smile turned wonderfully wicked as he took a step closer to her and reached out to unbutton the top button of her blouse. His gaze remained intent and heavy on hers as he slowly—so slowly—undid each button of the blouse. Noelle's whole body thrummed with excitement and expectation as she felt Ammar's fingers whisper down her body. She didn't move, didn't touch him, because she knew instinctively that Ammar was leading this dance and she was his willing and waiting partner.

With the final button undone he carefully parted her blouse and then let it slip from her shoulders. Noelle gave a tiny shrug and it slid to the ground. Deftly he unhooked her bra, and that followed the blouse to the floor.

He slid his hands along her shoulders and then cupped her breasts, his palms cradling their softness as his thumbs brushed across the achingly sensitised peaks. She let out a shuddering breath. 'Tell me what to do,' she whispered.

'Undress me.'

A thrill ran through her. She felt emboldened and powerful as she stepped closer to him and began to undo the buttons of his shirt. She felt him tremble under her touch and she fumbled with the button, laughing softly.

'My fingers are shaking.' In answer Ammar reached for her hand and placed it over his heart; she could feel it thunder in his chest. 'Mine, too,' she whispered, and undid another button. It seemed to take forever to undo them all, but finally she was sliding the shirt off his broad shoulders, glorying in the feel of sleek skin and hard muscle. She loved touching him. She'd been aching to do it for so long, and now that she could she felt like a child in a sweet shop, looking around in wonder. *Hers.* He was all hers.

His shirt fell to the floor and she gazed at his bare chest, the sprinkling of dark hair veeing down to the waistband of his trousers, the sculpted muscles and taut lines of his beautiful body. 'Now what?' she asked shakily.

'Round two,' Ammar murmured, and icy heat raced through her as he reached for the button of her skirt and popped it open with his thumb. Just the brush of his fingers against her bare tummy sent another blaze of desire shooting through her, and she swayed on her feet as he unzipped and slid the skirt down her legs, falling to his knees in front of her.

'Ammar...'

He slid his hand down the length of her bare leg, his touch sure and possessive, and then balanced her with his other hand as he helped her to step out of her skirt. Undressing, Noelle thought hazily, had never taken so long nor felt so erotic.

Then she stopped thinking at all as Ammar hooked his thumbs in the waistband of her knickers and slowly slid those down her legs as well, so she was completely naked.

He slid his hands back up her legs to her hips, cradling her surely as he arched her pelvis towards him. Noelle's eyes fluttered closed as he pressed a kiss at the juncture of her thighs, one little kiss that still sent waves of pleasure pulsating through her. Then he righted her again and stood up.

'Now me.'

Noelle eyed his belt buckle and trouser zip with a dazed scepticism, for her fingers were trembling so much she wasn't sure she'd be able to manage any of it. Her whole body was trembling, shaking with the force of her desire for him.

'This might take a while,' she joked, and Ammar smiled.

'I told you we weren't rushing.'

Noelle reached for his belt buckle, fumbling with it helplessly. 'For a woman who specialises in accessories, you don't know your way around a belt very well,' he admonished wryly, and she gave a soft laugh.

'I'm hopeless.'

Ammar wrapped his fingers around hers, stilling them

on his belt. 'Nothing about this,' he said quietly, 'is hopeless.'

Noelle felt a lump rise in her throat. 'You're right,' she whispered. This moment was full of hope and wonder and love. She felt dizzy with it all. 'Still,' she managed, 'I'd like to get your trousers off.'

'I'd like that, too.'

He smiled at her, his expression so full of desire and love that Noelle felt a flare of joyful power and quickly she undid his belt, unzipped his trousers. She slid his trousers down his legs and then glanced at his boxers, his arousal gloriously evident. Ammar caught her chin in his fingers and she realised she'd been staring.

'Touch me,' he said softly, and she slid his boxers off and wrapped her hand around the hard, silky length of his erection. 'Oh, Noelle,' he said with a shuddering breath. 'I love you.'

She let out a choked cry, overwhelmed by the poignancy and even sacredness of the moment. Ammar drew her to him, her naked body so wonderfully pressed against his, every point in exquisite and aching contact.

Then Ammar led her to the huge bed with its silk duvet and laid her down as gently and reverently as a treasure. He joined her and they lay there for a moment, unspeaking, the only sound the soft draw and sigh of their breathing. Slowly he slid his hand over her body, smoothing her skin from shoulder to hip. Noelle lifted her own hand and did the same, loving the feel of him, revelling in the freedom she felt in touching him.

Ammar drew her to him for a deep, lingering kiss that turned hungry, demanding, the intensity of their desire taking them over. He pulled her to him, his hands roving over her as he kissed her again, just as deeply, and Noelle hooked one leg around his, felt the insistent brush of his arousal against her and arched towards him.

Neither of them spoke, but no words were needed. There was just this, the brush of lips and fingers, the soft sigh of surrender and pleasure. Noelle's hands curled around the taut muscles of Ammar's shoulders as he finally, wondrously slid inside her. He paused, and in that silent moment Noelle knew they were both overwhelmed by the sense of completion and wholeness the joining of their bodies had brought.

She wrapped her legs around his hips and arched upwards, accepting him even more fully as Ammar began to move with smooth, sure strokes. Noelle found his rhythm and matched it, their bodies working sinuously and sensuously together, and as pleasure surged through her, spiralling upwards and upwards, she cried out his name and buried her head in the curve of his shoulder, racked by sudden, helpless sobs of joy.

Sunlight streamed through the crack between the curtains of Ammar's bedroom and with a sudden scraping sound he opened them, letting the hard lemon-yellow light bathe the room with its brightness.

Noelle rolled over in the bed, felt the yawning empty space next to her as she stretched. She felt wonderfully sated, her whole body filled with a wonderful languor even as it pulsed with the memory of last night. Neither of them had got much sleep.

Ammar glanced back at her now, eyebrows raised. He seemed, Noelle thought, more relaxed than she'd ever seen him. His chest was bare, a pair of drawstring trousers riding low on his hips so she could see the hard ridge of bone and taut muscle. He looked, as always, mouth-dryingly gorgeous.

'Sleep well?' he asked, and she gave a little laugh.

'I don't think I slept much at all.'

His mouth curved in a knowing smile. 'Funny, I didn't, either.'

She pushed a tangle of hair away from her eyes, wanting to ask him to come back to bed, but the words caught in her throat. Last night had been wonderful, but she still felt strangely shy this morning. He came anyway, sitting on the edge as he glanced at her solemnly.

'It's Sunday.'

'Is it?' The weekend had flown by, and yet at the same time Noelle felt as if she'd been here for ever. A lifetime lived in the space of a few days.

'You need to go back to Paris.'

She stared at him, not wanting to grasp the implication. 'I do?'

'From the horrified look on your face, I take it you've come to appreciate desert living.'

'I suppose I have.'

'But needs must,' he said, rising from the bed. 'I'd hate to cost you your job.'

Her job. Noelle sank back against the pillows. She hadn't given Arche even a thought for at least twenty-four hours. After two days' unexplained absence, she wasn't even sure she'd have a job left. She could definitely forget about the promotion. Why didn't she care? Because, she realised with a pang, she had never loved the job in the first place. She'd tried to and she'd poured her life in it, the new life she'd created post-Ammar that bore no resemblance to the person she'd been with him, the person she wanted to be now. Her true self. *When I'm with him,* she thought, *I'm the woman I want to be.*

'I have some work to do in the Paris office anyway,' Ammar said, distracting her as he reached for a T-shirt and slid it over his head. Noelle watched the sculpted muscles of his chest disappear beneath the white cotton with a flicker of regret. 'We can fly out this afternoon.'

'We'll both go?'

'That's the idea.'

It was a wonderful idea, Noelle thought. A normal and yet intoxicating idea—living in the same city, sharing simple pleasures. They'd go on dates. They'd watch films and eat take-away and sleep—what little sleep they might get—in the same bed.

A few hours later, they took a helicopter to Marrakech, touching down at the airport only to board a private plane that would take them to Paris. Noelle settled into a sumptuous sofa of cream leather with a sigh of appreciation.

'Do you always take a private jet, wherever you go?' she asked.

'Yes.' Ammar sat across from her and opened his briefcase.

'It must be an awful expense.'

He took a sheaf of papers out. 'It's worth it.'

There was something repressive about his manner, the way he wouldn't look at her. Noelle felt a flicker of unease. She knew he didn't like to talk about Tannous Enterprises. She didn't really like to ask. But, sitting there across from him, she was conscious of how much she didn't know. 'You said you wanted to legitimise Tannous Enterprises,' she said quietly. 'What does that mean exactly?'

'Exactly what it sounds like.' Ammar was still scanning his papers, clearly unwilling to look her in the eye or continue this conversation.

Noelle reached over and laid a hand across the papers he was reading so avidly, causing him to look up, startled. 'Don't,' she said quietly. 'Don't shut me out.'

He stared at her for a long moment, and Noelle could

not read his expression at all. She hated it when he blanked her out like this, almost as if he were blanking himself out. Not thinking anything, just as he'd told her before. 'I'm not shutting you out,' he said evenly. 'But I'm not sure you want to know all the sordid details of my father's business. He was corrupt, Noelle. A criminal.' He spoke flatly, his jaw tight.

Noelle swallowed. 'But it's your business now.'

'Exactly.'

'Are they so very sordid?' she asked, heard how small her voice sounded. Ammar uncapped a gold-plated pen and made a notation on one of the papers.

'It's simply not worth discussing. I intend to legalise every aspect of Tannous Enterprises and make restitution where it is necessary.'

Doing what was right. 'That sounds like a huge job.'

'It is.'

She felt a surge of admiration for what he was undertaking, what he wanted to do. Impulsively, she leaned over and placed her hand on his. His skin was warm, his muscles taut. 'I'm proud of you, Ammar. Of what you're doing.'

He glanced at her properly, his amber eyes opaque and fathomless. A muscle jerked in his jaw. 'Don't speak too soon,' he said, and removed his hand. 'I haven't done much of anything yet.'

'But you will.' She spoke with confidence, with love, and she knew Ammar heard it. He glanced at her again and she saw a hunger in his eyes, a need she felt bloom in herself. Suddenly she was breathless.

Slowly he reached one hand out and laced his fingers with hers. Her heart began to pound as he drew her to him, up from her seat and across the aisle and then onto his lap, her legs splayed across his hips. She felt the hard ridge of his erection against her and a thrill ran through, like icy fire.

He tangled his hands in her hair, drew her face to him for a kiss so deep and endless it felt as if he were plumbing the depths of her soul. She pressed against him, let out a shuddering breath as he pressed back, every point of contact aching with exquisite and unsated desire.

He slid his hands under her top and nudged aside her bra, his palms cupping her breasts as he shifted to angle her more purposefully on top of him. Another thrill shot through her at the feeling of him underneath her, and she let out a shuddering breath. She would never get tired of this, never feel that she had enough of him.

Ammar flipped open the top button of her skirt, the flat of his hand sliding along her skin. Noelle instinctively wriggled her hips to give him greater access. Yet, just as his fingers tugged beneath the lace of her underwear, the sound of a door opening, a throat clearing had them both freezing.

'Excuse me, sir—' One of Ammar's staff dropped his voice to a horrified hush. 'I'm sorry; I just wanted to let you know we're ready for take-off—'

'Indeed,' Ammar said dryly. 'I certainly am,' he murmured in Noelle's ear, and she buried her face in the warm curve of his shoulder, her own shoulders shaking with sudden laughter.

With another murmured apology, the man left and Noelle lifted her head from Ammar's shoulder. 'I'm so embarrassed.'

'You're gorgeous. And, fortunately for us, this plane comes with a bedroom.'

'We couldn't—' Noelle protested, and he gave her a wicked smile.

'Oh, yes, we could.'
And they did.

Ammar couldn't keep from smiling even as he tried to
focus on the papers in front of him. He glanced up at
Noelle, saw her curled up across from him, one hand resting against her cheek as she read a fashion magazine, a
faint frown puckering her forehead. They'd made good
use of that bedroom and his body still thrummed with the
satisfaction of making Noelle his again. Having her say
she was proud of him had been an overwhelming aphrodi-
siac. Hearing the love in her voice, knowing she believed
in him—

She doesn't know anything.

The thought slammed into his mind with the force of
a hammer, shattering the hope that had been buoying his
heart and taking the smile off his face. Ammar closed his
eyes in silent supplication, willing himself not to think
even as the happiness he'd just felt evaporated in the hard
light of reality. Noelle didn't know a damn thing about
what he'd done. What he'd been capable of.

And some day she would have to find out.

Don't think about it. He forced his mind to blank. *Don't
think, don't remember. You're different now. With Noelle
by your side, you can be different.*

To his surprise, he felt the soft touch of her hand on his
and he looked up to see her smiling at him, although her
eyes were dark and troubled. 'Don't worry so much,' she
said quietly, and squeezed his hand. Ammar captured her
hand in his and brought it to his lips.

'I'm not,' he lied, smiling as he kissed her fingers. She
smiled back, so very trusting. Believing in him. He felt
that hard knot of worry ease, just a little. With Noelle by

his side—and in his bed—everything would be different. He would be.

Several hours later, they landed in Paris. A limousine with darkly tinted windows was waiting for them at the gate and Ammar ushered her in while one of his local team went for their bags. Her eyes widened at the sight of the two dark-suited men going about their business with cold, brisk efficiency.

His driver, Youssef, spoke to him in Arabic, asking him if he wanted to go directly to the corporate penthouse his father had always kept in Paris. Noelle frowned as he answered back before turning to her. 'I'll drop you off before I go to my apartment.'

'I thought,' she said, 'you'd stay with me.'

If only it could be so simple. 'Work prevents me from doing so.'

'Work?'

Ammar felt himself tense. He wanted to keep Noelle as separate from work as possible, at least until he'd swept Tannous Enterprises clean. 'I have many meetings, commitments,' he explained, trying to keep his voice mild. 'I'm reorganising every regional branch of the company, going through records and files, interviewing staff. Firing people as well. It is time-consuming and somewhat unpleasant, and I don't wish to bring such things into your home.'

'I see.'

Noelle turned to stare out of the window, the Parisian traffic sliding by, and Ammar wondered just what she thought she saw. Was he imagining the flicker of suspicion in her eyes, just because he felt it himself?

Pushing the pointless thought away, he took out his smartphone and sent a few texts to various members of his staff. He didn't want to concern Noelle with any of it, didn't want her to worry or even to know, yet he feared he was attempting the impossible—on far too many levels. Tannous Enterprises was the elephant in the room with them, the camel with its great hulking nose under the tent. The only way to get rid of it would be to acknowledge it, explain everything, and Ammar wasn't willing to do that. Not yet. Not when this thing between them was so new, so fragile. So untested.

At her apartment building on the Ile St-Louis he instructed Youssef to wait while he escorted her upstairs. Noelle glanced back at the burly man standing in front of her building, his arms crossed.

'Who's that?'

'One of my security team. His name is Ahmed.'

'Why is he there?'

'To protect us.'

She shook her head slowly. 'I didn't realise we needed protecting. You didn't have a security team in the desert, did you?'

'No, but I didn't need one. It's miles from anywhere.' They'd reached the top floor and Noelle slowly unlocked the door to her apartment, her forehead wrinkled in a frown.

'I don't like it.'

'I should tell you, I intend to keep Ahmed with you,' Ammar said as she opened the door. 'For your own protection.'

She dropped her keys on the hall table and turned to him, eyebrows raised, expression guarded. 'Do you actually think I'm in some kind of danger?'

'No,' he answered swiftly, 'but it would ease my mind, and I have no intention of taking any risks with you.'

'What kind of risks?'

Ammar thought of some of the people he'd dealt with and shook his head. 'Noelle, I was able to have you taken from your doorstep without anyone even noticing. I simply want you to be protected.'

Her expression darkened, like a cloud had come over the sun. He shouldn't have mentioned that, he realised. Reminded her of what he'd done. 'That was you,' she said quietly. 'Am I in danger from you, Ammar?'

Ammar felt as if he'd been punched in the chest. He felt, quite literally, breathless, no more so than when she gazed at him sorrowfully. It had been a genuine question. She was still waiting for the answer.

'Do you think you are?' he asked, his voice no more than a rough thread of sound.

She stared at him and the soft line of her mouth trembled. 'No,' she said at last, but it had taken her at least ten seconds to reply. Ammar drew a ragged breath into his lungs. All the euphoric hope he'd been feeling at knowing she loved him, believed in him, leaked out of him, left him flat.

'I see,' he said quietly, and she bit her lip.

'Ammar, I know I'm not in danger from you. Not…not the kind of danger that requires a bodyguard, at any rate.'

'What kind of danger are you talking about, then?' he asked evenly.

Her eyes were luminous as she stared at him, her lip still caught between her teeth. 'Nothing,' she whispered, but he knew what she wasn't saying. Of course he did. She was afraid he would abandon her again. Reject and hurt her, just as he had before.

Every instinct in him reared up, urged him to cloak himself in cold anger. But he was different now, he wanted to be different, and so with effort he said, 'I would never do anything to hurt you, Noelle. *Never*.'

'I know you wouldn't,' she whispered, but again he knew what she wasn't saying. *You wouldn't mean to.*

'I love you,' he said, the words like jagged pieces cutting him up inside. He knew he sounded reluctant, grudging, but he meant every word. It was just so hard to say them. 'Come here,' he commanded gruffly and, with her eyes wide and dark, a frown still wrinkling her forehead, she slowly walked over to him. Ammar closed the last few inches, his hands curling around her shoulders, drawing her pliant softness to him. He leaned his forehead against hers, her hair whispering against his face, and breathed in the sweet feminine scent of her. 'I love you,' he said again, and this time it sounded better. As if he meant it, and was maybe even happy about it.

She let out a trembling laugh. 'Does it get easier the more you say it?'

'A little bit.' She didn't answer, but he saw a tear form at the corner of her eye. 'Oh, please, don't,' he muttered. He couldn't bear the thought that he was still making her cry. 'Don't.' And then he kissed her, brushing her lips softly against his, his thumbs catching the dampness of her tears.

She kissed him back softly, a promise. 'I'm sorry,' she whispered. 'I have my own ghosts, Ammar. My own memories and fears. It's not just you that has to learn to be different.'

He'd never thought Noelle needed to change, yet it humbled him now to know she was trying, just like he was. Trying to trust. Wanting to love.

'We'll help each other,' he said gruffly. He was still unused to these words, these conversations. So much emotion, so much painful honesty. As gently as he could, he eased away from her. 'I should go. I have business to attend to.' She nodded, her face shadowed once more, questions in her eyes. 'Have dinner with me tonight,' he said, and her expression lightened, if only a little.

'OK.'

He stared at her, words crowding his throat, words he was still afraid to say. He loved her; she loved him. Why couldn't it be simple?

Everything still felt difficult, impossible even, insurmountable obstacles strewn across the twisting path to their happiness. Secrets. Sins. Sorrows and fears.

And when those emerged into the harsh and revealing light of day, Ammar wondered bleakly, what would be left? Would Noelle still love him? Would she even look at him?

He was afraid to answer that question.

With a jerky nod of farewell, he turned and left.

CHAPTER NINE

'NOT that one.'

Noelle glanced back in amused surprise as Ammar issued his directive. She'd been about to select an haute couture gown in silvery-grey from the rack of dresses the shop assistant had brought forward, but paused when he shook his head. 'What's wrong with it?'

'Too dark.'

'Too *dark*?' The dress shimmered with subtle silver threads.

'How about a bright colour?'

Noelle pursed her lips. 'Bright colours aren't fashionable.'

'I thought you predicted fashion,' Ammar pointed out all too reasonably, and Noelle let out a little laugh.

'I do, but—' She stepped back, arms crossed. 'I don't think there's a bright colour in this whole boutique.'

'Then let's go somewhere else.'

She glanced at him speculatively; he was stretched out on a cream leather divan, looking intensely masculine, even in this feminine and fussy little boutique. She'd asked him to attend a charity gala with her that evening, their first public outing together since returning to Paris, and Ammar had agreed on one condition: she had to buy a new dress.

Noelle had laughed, insisting she had plenty of dresses already, but Ammar had been just as insistent. He wanted to buy her a dress. And she was happy to humour him; she loved seeing him smile, looking relaxed. This last week in Paris had been full of such moments, smiles and kisses and sudden shared laughter. Every joyful moment felt like a miracle, a wonder.

She'd seen him almost every day, and most definitely every night. Her body ached with the joyful exhaustion of many nights spent awash with pleasure. Even now, everything in her tightened with both longing and anticipation at the thought of the night ahead, when the charity gala ended and Ammar took her back to her apartment, and then to her bedroom, and to her bed. He'd strip the dress—whichever one she chose—slowly from her body, taking his time, torturing her with expectation, smiling all the while that slow, sleepy smile she'd come to know and love. And then—

'Noelle?'

She felt her body jolt in surprise and turned to smile at him, felt a telltale flush flood her face. From the glint in Ammar's amber eyes, she suspected he knew the nature of her thoughts. 'Sorry—what were you saying?'

'Another boutique?'

She was still blushing. 'Yes, all right.'

They walked down the Champs-Elysées and Ammar reached for her hand, threading his fingers through hers. These small gestures, which would have been so hard a few weeks ago, now came, if not naturally, then more easily. Everything he did was deliberate, a choice. He chose her, and Noelle loved him all the more for it.

'Let's go in this one,' he said, and pointed to a tiny shop crowded with dresses in a rainbow of colours. Noelle looked at it dubiously; she'd never been in it and normally wouldn't give it a second glance.

'All right,' she said, and slipped into the small boutique. Ammar strode ahead of her, pushing aside racks of dresses with such authority that Noelle could have laughed. She never would have expected him to take an interest in women's fashion.

'This one,' he said, and withdrew the most ridiculous dress Noelle had ever seen. Bubblegum-pink, strapless with ruffled tiers falling in flounces to the floor, it was an outrageous meringue of a dress, and something she'd never, ever wear.

'Ammar—'

He glanced at her over the ruffles, his eyes glinting mischievously. 'Please.'

Laughing in both exasperation and amusement, she grabbed the dress from him. 'Fine. But it will look ridiculous.'

Strangely, it didn't. Noelle stared at her reflection, amazed that the flouncy pink ruffles somehow worked. She wouldn't have been caught dead in a dress like this for years. Ever since she'd started working for Arche, started being thin and glamorous and hard-nosed. The person she'd wanted to become, even if it had never been who she really was.

'Noelle?' Ammar tapped on the dressing room door. 'How ridiculous is it?'

'It's not ridiculous at all.' She swallowed past the sudden lump in her throat. She looked more like herself in this dress than she could have ever imagined. Her face was softer, her colour higher, her eyes brighter. She looked… happy. Happier than she had in a long, long time.

'May I see it?' he asked, and she opened the door.

Ammar stared at her for a long moment without speaking, without any expression at all. Noelle felt her heart seem to stop right in her chest. 'Do you like it?' she whispered and he took both her hands in his.

'You're unbearably beautiful,' he said, and she let out a little laugh as she twirled around, self-conscious and yet beaming.

'I feel like Cinderella.'

'You wanted a Cinderella dress, didn't you?'

She stopped mid-twirl, her heart slamming in her chest. She'd forgotten she'd said that, but he hadn't. 'Yes,' she said, 'I did.'

He smiled and, reaching for her hand, helped her to finish the twirl. Her dress flared out around her, a swirl of candy-pink. 'Then be Cinderella for an evening. And at midnight I'll take you home.' His eyes darkened, his gaze heavy on hers and Noelle knew he was imagining how the evening would end. They'd made love every night since coming to Paris, and yet it still wasn't enough. She still felt the heady thrill of anticipation at the thought of spending another night in his arms.

'As long as your car won't turn into a pumpkin,' she quipped, and went back into the dressing room to change.

Ammar arranged for the dress to be delivered to her apartment, and they wandered back into the summer sunshine. It was a beautiful day, the air drowsy and warm, Paris at its best, full of tourists and lovers. They stopped at a pavement café overlooking the Seine, everything bathed in lemony light.

'I want to show you something, after this,' Ammar said, and Noelle looked up in surprise.

'You can spare the afternoon, as well as the evening?' she asked, stirring her coffee. She took milk now, and one sugar.

Ammar gave a small smile. 'I am the boss, after all.'

'But you're not too busy—with your meetings?'

'I decide the meetings.' Ammar took a sip of his own coffee, the simple movement somehow repressive. He didn't, Noelle knew, want to talk about his work. He never did. She wished he would share more of it, wanted to help and support him, yet any time she asked he always shut the conversation down, kindly but firmly. Clearly work was off-limits, and Noelle could understand why; it was a messy, unpleasant business, restoring Tannous Enterprises, righting so many wrongs. She still wanted to be a part of it, and every part of Ammar's life, but she recognised she needed to be patient. Ammar had given so much of himself already; he would give that, too, eventually. She had to believe that.

'So where are we going now?' she asked as they left the café and began walking towards the narrow cobbled streets of Paris's Latin Quarter.

'Oh, just a little place I know,' Ammar said, sounding so nonchalant Noelle immediately wondered what he had planned. Ammar didn't *do* nonchalance. Everything was deliberate.

Still holding her hand, he led her down one narrow street after another, past tiny pavement cafés and shops, bakeries with baskets of baguettes out front and patisseries with trays of glossy strawberry-topped tarts.

Then he stopped suddenly in front of a shop that, as far as Noelle could tell, was abandoned. Its front window was dusty and empty and peeling gold letters on the crooked, creaking sign indicated that it had once sold women's shoes.

'If you're worried about whether I have shoes to match the dress, I don't think this is the place to go,' she joked, but Ammar didn't answer her, just slipped a key out of his pocket.

'Here we are.' With a little rattling he opened the door to the shop and ushered Noelle into its dim, dusty interior. 'You need to use your imagination, of course,' he said, 'but what do you think?'

'What do I *think?*' Noelle stifled a sneeze. 'It's… Well, it's…' She stopped helplessly. 'What is it?'

Ammar chuckled softly. 'It's nothing but an old empty shop right now, obviously. But, as for what it could be—your bookshop, of course.'

'My…' She trailed off, suddenly seeing the empty space with its dust and rubbish in a completely new way. 'My bookshop,' she repeated. 'I didn't even think you remembered—'

'I remembered.' He pointed to the window. 'Armchairs in the window so people can read in the sun. Paintings on the wall, local work by aspiring artists. And you wanted a little café as well, didn't you—selling brioche and croissants and, of course, coffee.'

'Yes,' she whispered. 'Yes, that's exactly how I imagined it.'

'The place is for rent now that the last business went bankrupt. The owner doesn't want to sell, but a five-year lease is reasonable.' He raised his eyebrows. 'What do you think?'

'I think,' Noelle said slowly, 'that you're wonderful.'

He raised his eyebrows. '*I'm* wonderful?'

'Yes. For remembering what I said. What I wanted. And helping me to make it happen.' She crossed the shop and stood on tiptoe to kiss his cheek. 'That means so much to me, Ammar.' She knew he could have bought her a huge boutique on the Champs-Elysées. It would have been a negligible sum to him, and yet he hadn't. It wasn't about the money, or even the shop. It was about him knowing what her dreams were and wanting to make them real.

'Thank you,' she whispered, and this time she brushed her lips against his.

Ammar drew her to him, deepened the kiss. 'We could,' he suggested huskily, 'christen the shop.'

Noelle let out a little laugh even as a thrill ran through her. Already Ammar was sliding his hand under her skirt, his palm warm and firm on her hip. She pressed against him, desire racing through her veins, igniting deep inside her.

'We could,' she murmured against his mouth, and kissed him again. Ammar tightened his hands on her hips, guiding her to cradle his arousal. Noelle let out a shuddering breath. Somehow, in the space of a few seconds, it stopped being a playful exchange and turned into something raw and urgent. Ammar backed her up against the wall, his mouth relentless and demanding on hers as he hooked her leg around his waist. Noelle pulled him closer, her breath coming in panting gasps as she gave him kiss for kiss, demand for demand.

In a distant, hazy part of her brain a voice reminded her that the door wasn't locked and people could stroll by the shop, or even come in. It didn't matter. All she could feel and think and *know* was Ammar. Ammar's hands on her skin, his lips on hers. Ammar inside her, loving her, knowing her.

Afterwards, she sagged against the wall, Ammar still holding her, her legs trembling, her heart pounding. She wiped a strand of hair from her face.

'Wow,' she said shakily, and Ammar grinned.

'Wow, indeed,' he murmured.

By the time she returned to her apartment, the dress had been delivered. She unwrapped it and gazed at the pink flounces in a sort of dazed joy, because the dress was ridiculous and yet she loved it. She loved that Ammar had chosen it for her, loved that she was becoming the woman she'd always meant to be with him.

And tonight she'd be Cinderella.

Two hours later, she entered the opulent ballroom of one of Paris's best hotels on Ammar's arm. She felt as if she stood out like a vibrant flower in a stark winter garden, her pink dress the only splash of colour in a sea of black.

Ammar slipped his arm around her waist. 'You're gorgeous,' he whispered, 'and every woman here is wishing she could pull off a pink dress.'

Noelle let out a little bubble of laughter. She felt light and free and so, so happy; she felt as if she could float right up to the ceiling. Ammar squeezed her hand, and she squeezed his back.

They moved among the glittering guests and Noelle made introductions when necessary, her heart swelling with pride at being on his arm, by his side. She was so lost in her own haze of happiness that she didn't notice at first the way some people greeted Ammar with terse nods, their gazes speculative or sliding away.

Yet after a while she did notice, and she saw the grim cast of Ammar's face, the rigid set of his shoulders. The way people looked as if they were almost afraid of him. The thought seemed ridiculous, and yet with an icy pang she realised it wasn't. Ammar was a powerful man, yet what did she really know about that power? She knew he was trying to legitimise Tannous Enterprises, but she still didn't understand what that meant. What had happened in the past.

What Ammar had done.

She'd heard enough whispers over the years, scanned the articles on websites and in newspapers. She'd avoided most of it because she'd never wanted even to hear the name Tannous again, but she couldn't ignore it completely.

Could not forget what Ammar himself had said, when she'd first seen him. When he'd kidnapped her.

I've done too many things already I could be arrested for. One more won't matter.

Impatient with herself, Noelle pushed the thoughts away. Why was she thinking of this now? Ammar was different now. She was different. She wanted to enjoy this evening, to remain in her haze of happiness. Yet every guarded sideways look, every sudden silence pierced that protective bubble and brought the old memories and fears slinking back. Reminded her of how much she still didn't know.

She glanced at him, her arm still laced with his; he looked magnificent in his tuxedo, a tall, imposing figure, every inch of him exuding power. And yet she found herself looking at him as she would someone she didn't know.

Who is this man?

He turned to her, his eyes narrowed with concern. 'Are you cold?'

She realised she'd shivered. She shook her head. Even so, Ammar put his arm around her shoulders, pulled her closer to him. Noelle closed her eyes briefly, savouring the contact. The comfort and the reassurance.

I love this man.

Surely that was all that mattered.

Midway through the evening, Amelie found her. 'You're here with Mr Scary, aren't you?' she crowed in delight, and Noelle shook her head.

'Don't call him that.'

'He's too, too sexy,' Amelie said, turning to gaze at Ammar from across the room. 'I heard he survived a helicopter crash.'

'Where did you hear that?'

'Gossip.' Amelie shrugged. 'Everyone's curious, you

know.' She glanced at Noelle, her expression shrewdly speculative. 'Is that why you missed work last week? A dirty weekend?'

'No.' Not exactly. She swallowed, wishing she could ease the tightness in her chest. In her heart.

'Aren't you Little Miss Coy?' Amelie gave a salacious smile. 'Well, I'd do him. He's gorgeous.'

Jealousy flared through her, even though she knew it was absurd. 'He's off-limits, Amelie.'

'Not to you, obviously.'

Yes, to me. The thought caught her on the raw. Ammar had been so open with her about so many things. How could she demand more? And yet she knew there were things he wasn't telling her. Things she needed—and yet was afraid—to know. 'I think I'll use the Ladies,' she said, and she slipped past Amelie to the sumptuous powder room off the foyer of the hotel.

Alone, she stared at her reflection in the mirror. Her face was pale, her eyes huge, her mouth a thin, pressed line. She glanced down at her pink dress, remembered how happy Ammar had been to see her in it. How happy she'd felt wearing it. Like Cinderella, only now the clock had struck midnight and it felt as if it had all turned to pumpkins and rags.

She gripped the scalloped edge of the washbasin and closed her eyes, willing to feel just a little bit of that joy. *I love him. He loves me. When I'm with him, I'm the woman I want to be.*

She needed to be that woman now.

She sucked in a desperate breath, let it out slowly. She knew Ammar would be wondering where she was. She needed to find him, to be with him. *Just be.*

She ran water into the basin and wet her wrists, dabbed

her eyes and took a deep breath. Resolutely, she turned towards the door.

She'd only taken a few steps out into the deserted foyer when a voice, strained and high-pitched, stopped her in her stilettos.

'You're with him, aren't you?'

Slowly Noelle turned around, saw a young woman with a pale face and angry eyes glaring at her. Her mind and body felt frozen, so she could barely form a coherent thought.

'Who are you talking about?' she asked, even though she knew all too well just who the woman was talking about.

'Tannous.' She spat his name, made it sound like a curse. 'He ruined my father.'

Noelle stared, everything inside her still frozen. She knew, in a distant part of her brain, that she should walk away. She surely didn't want to hear this, not from some angry stranger. Whatever truth needed telling should come from Ammar. Yet somehow she found her mouth opening, her lips forming one word. 'How?'

'Tannous Enterprises bought the company my father worked for,' the woman said, every word punctuated with pain. 'They transferred all the employees' pensions to life insurance policies.'

Noelle shook her head, not understanding. She even felt the first flicker of relief, the realisation that the secrets she knew Ammar must be hiding might not be so bad after all.

'The life insurance policies were worthless,' the woman explained bitterly. 'The company went bust, just as Tannous knew it would all along, since he'd sold it. And meanwhile he drained the pension funds. Every single employee was left with nothing, not even a legal leg to stand on.'

Noelle shook her head again. 'But—'

'Tannous got away with it, of course. He always does. He has a smarmy lawyer who keeps him out of trouble. And my father had nothing. He died two months ago from a heart attack, a broken man.'

Noelle closed her eyes briefly. 'I'm very sorry for your loss,' she whispered.

'Are you?' the woman challenged. 'Ammar Tannous is completely immoral, totally corrupt, and Tannous Enterprises is rotten to the core. If he weren't so damn rich he'd be in jail. So why are you with him?' The question rang out through the foyer, both demand and challenge, and Noelle froze. Said nothing. The woman waited, clearly expecting an answer. *Why are you with him?* Noelle just shook her head. Slowly, every part of her leaden, she walked away.

The rest of the evening passed in a fog. She saw Ammar give her a sharp glance when she returned and knew she must look…something. Pale. Tired. *Devastated.*

Who are you? What things have you done?

Somehow she dragged herself through the endless rounds of chit-chat, meaningless conversations and laughter and gossip. She wasn't even aware of what she was saying, much less what came out of anyone's mouth.

I love you. I still love you.

Her heart cried out, but everything in her resisted. *I can't do this. I don't even know this man. I don't know what he's done, what he's capable of.*

She told herself she'd known this, some part of her had understood, on a basic, vague level, that Ammar had done things like this. Immoral, illegal, criminal things. And she knew he was different now, *wanted* to be different, and yet she had never imagined how it would feel. To know, and yet not to know at the same time, just what he'd done. Who he was.

She didn't actually speak to Ammar until they were speeding away from the hotel in his blacked-out limousine, Youssef at the wheel.

Ammar stared out of the window, every angle of his body hard and uncompromising, his face turned away from her. 'Someone said something to you, didn't they?'

And the fact that he knew, that there even *was* something to be said, made everything inside her curl into a tight, protective ball. Her vision blurred and she swallowed hard. 'Yes.' He didn't answer, and Noelle forced out, 'Don't you want to know what it was?'

Ammar did not move his gaze from the window. 'Not particularly.'

She looked away. The tension in the car felt thick, choking. It hurt to breathe. It hurt to think. She closed her eyes, willed Ammar to say something, *anything* to make it OK again. If he just touched her, turned his face towards her—

The car pulled up to her building. Ammar had spent most nights here and, although he'd never said it, Noelle thought he preferred her cosy home to the sterile luxury of his corporate penthouse. Now she slid out of the car on leaden legs, felt Ammar's presence heavy behind her as they took the old lift with its wrought iron grille up to the sixth floor. She tried to unlock her door, but her fingers trembled around the key and it clattered to the floor.

Ammar picked it up. 'Let me,' he said, and unlocked the door, ushering her in first before he came in and closed it behind him. Neither of them spoke.

Noelle wished he would say something. *Anything*. Anything to break this terrible silence that grew worse with every endless moment it stretched on. Finally she managed to whisper, 'Why don't you want to know?'

Ammar stared at her impassively. 'Why don't I want to know what?'

'What…what was said to me.' His face remained expressionless and she knew he was blanking her out again, and she couldn't bear it. 'Aren't you the tiniest bit curious, Ammar? Obviously it affected me. Upset me.'

'I can see that.'

'And so?'

'And so what?' He flexed one hand, the gesture dismissive. 'Something was said, you were upset. Why do I need to know what it was?'

'Because…because then you could explain it to me!'

'You didn't understand?'

She let out a choked breath. She didn't think she'd ever seen Ammar seem so…indifferent. Even when he'd been rejecting her, there had been a storm in his eyes. Torment. She only realised now how conflicted he must have been then. He hadn't been as coldly certain as this.

'I did understand,' she whispered. 'At least, I think I did. But I just didn't…I didn't think…'

'You didn't think I'd done it?'

Miserably she stared at him. 'I don't know.'

Ammar stared back, his expression an assessment as his gaze roved coldly over her. 'Well, I did do it,' he said and she blinked.

'I didn't even tell you what it was.'

'It doesn't matter.'

'How can you say that?'

He shrugged. 'Because whatever someone's accused me of, it's likely I did it. And if I didn't, then I did enough and worse. So it really doesn't matter what it was, Noelle, because it always would have been something.'

She sank down heavily onto a chair; she felt as if her

legs wouldn't support her anymore. 'Why didn't you tell me this before?'

'What do you want, a laundry list?' His breath came out in an impatient hiss. 'In any case, I did tell you. I told you my father was a criminal; you knew I worked for him. I worked for him for nearly twenty years, Noelle. Do you really think, in all that time, I never got my hands dirty?'

She closed her eyes. 'No.' She didn't think that, not any more. And she recognised that she'd let herself not think it, not think of anything about Ammar's work, because it was easier to pretend it didn't matter. It didn't exist. It was at least partly her fault that it had come to this.

Ammar didn't speak, and she opened her eyes. He still looked impassive, almost bored, and she could not escape the terrible fear that she really didn't know him at all— because she hadn't wanted to know.

She wished he would take her in his arms, tell her how much he'd changed. She wished that would make a difference.

All she could think now was that there was twenty years of history between them, and it felt as if it had been completely rewritten. While she'd been a doe-eyed teen, dreaming of him, he'd been out in the world, going about his business, committing God only knew what kind of crimes. Even when they'd been dating—he'd been working then, his father's office in London. She remembered him saying something, changing the subject and she hadn't cared. She hadn't given it even a second of her thought.

She'd hadn't just been naïve, she'd been blind. Wilfully, stupidly blind, until tonight.

'Say something, Ammar,' she whispered.

'What do you want me to say?'

'I don't know.' She didn't know what would make it better, what would expel the doubt and shock and hurt from her heart. 'Tell me how it happened,' she finally said. 'Tell me how you came to work for your father like that.'

He stared at her and she couldn't tell a thing from his face. His eyes were dark and hard. 'I was his son.'

'But—'

'If you want me to tell you how he forced me into it, I can't.'

And she had been hoping for that, she knew. Some sort of excuse. Some way for her to say *I understand* and *It's OK then*. But there was nothing.

'Still,' she tried, 'you must have been a boy when you started—'

He let out a cold, hard laugh. 'You want to make excuses for me, Noelle, and there aren't any. I did what I did because I was my father's son. He commanded me, yes, but I liked having the kind of power he gave me. Seeing people stand to attention when I came into the room. Sometimes I even liked the fear I saw in their eyes.' He turned to stare out of the window, his whole body rigid.

She knew he was trying to shock her, to tell her the worst about himself, and it was working. She felt her mouth dry and her heart thud. 'Why did you stop, then?' she asked in a hoarse whisper. 'Why did you want to change?'

'Have I?' he asked softly, turning to fix her with a piercing gaze. 'Have I really changed at all?'

Noelle swallowed hard. Said nothing. The events of the evening had sapped all her strength, taken away her certainties. She couldn't face another confrontation, not now, when everything inside her felt twisted and tangled in knots of treacherous doubt.

'I think,' she whispered, 'I'd like to be alone tonight.'

Something flashed across Ammar's face, a lightning

streak of emotion, and then his expression blanked again. 'As you wish,' he said, and turned and walked out of her apartment.

Ammar rode in the lift to his penthouse alone. Anger pulsed through him, but underneath it he felt a deep ocean of despair, an overwhelming grief he could not let himself sink into. If he did, he'd never climb out of it again.

Yet just remembering that look of dazed disillusionment in Noelle's eyes made his heart pump and his fists clench. She'd found out about him.

It didn't matter what she'd heard, or even whether it was true or not. What mattered was she doubted him. Hell, maybe she even feared him.

She didn't—couldn't—love him.

The lift doors opened and Ammar strode into his apartment. His father's apartment, all modern chrome and glass. It had never felt like his. Nothing felt like his, except his house in the desert, an escape from everything...except who he was. He could never escape that.

He drove his fingers through his still-short hair, nails scraping skin, and longed for some release from all this emotion. All this anger and disappointment and pain. He didn't drink, so he couldn't lose himself in alcohol. He didn't smoke, had never done drugs, and sex, for tonight at least, was out of the question. He had, ironically, no vices.

And yet his life had been one of immorality, corruption and greed. His father's...and he'd carried out every order, if almost always with reluctance. There was no escaping that, not for him, not for Noelle.

It had been only a matter of time, he saw that now with stark, bleak clarity. Ten years ago he'd lost himself in the daydream of romance, the fairy tale of loving her. He'd listened to her talk about their happily-ever-after, her little bookshop, a house outside Paris, even children. He'd let himself be led along, bought into it all with a hope borne of desperation. He'd wanted it so much. And it was only after he'd said his vows that he realised what a sham it all was. *He* was. Fairy tales and happy endings were not, and never could be, for men like him.

He took a deep breath, forced himself to let it out slowly. *Don't think. Don't think about any of it.* He'd swim, he decided. Exercise had always been the best way to blank out his mind.

Yet even after a hundred hard laps in the penthouse pool his mind still seethed with memories. Noelle touching his face. Kissing his lips. Surrendering her body to his. Telling him she loved him.

I want to love you, Ammar.

What happened when she didn't want to any more?

This. This heartache, this loneliness and despair. It was surely no more than he should expect. No more than he deserved.

Resolutely, Ammar turned back to the pool for another hundred laps.

He worked through the night, too restless and edgy— and lonely—for sleep. He had, he realised, become used to sleeping with Noelle's soft body next to his, his arms around her. Amazing, really, considering until a few weeks ago he'd always slept alone. Lived alone, worked alone. He didn't have friends, or even colleagues. The only person in his whole life who had ever been close to him was Noelle.

The phone rang the next morning as he was drinking his second cup of black coffee.

'I saw you were out and about on the town last night.'

His brother Khalis's voice, laughing and light, came down the line. Ammar tensed, as a matter of instinct. For most of his life he'd been estranged from his brother.

They'd been playmates and best friends for those first few years, until his eighth birthday, when his father had called him into his study and hit him hard across the face. Showed him how things were going to be from now on, and being anyone's friend, even his brother's, wasn't part of that plan. And even though Ammar had, amazingly, reconciled with Khalis several weeks ago, a normal conversation still felt strange. Miraculous and bizarre, and he didn't always know what to say. Hell, he *never* knew what to say.

'Out and about?' he repeated guardedly.

'I read the social pages,' Khalis explained with a laugh. 'You were at some charity gala with a French woman— Ducasse?'

'Noelle.' Ammar's throat felt tight.

'She's beautiful,' Khalis said, and Ammar felt a totally unreasonable flare of jealousy. 'Is she who I think she is?' He'd told Khalis when they'd reconciled that he intended to find his wife. Make her his. Big words. Useless ones.

'Yes,' he said tightly.

His tone must have given it all away for Khalis gave a little sigh and said, 'So it's not going so well?'

'No.' It was all he could manage. It was more than he wanted to admit.

'What happened?'

Ammar gripped the phone so tightly his knuckles ached. 'She found out.'

'Found out?'

'About me.'

'What about you?'

'What do you think?' he snapped. His brother wasn't stupid, so Ammar had no idea why he was acting like he was. 'About Tannous Enterprises. About how corrupt it is.'

'Was,' Khalis corrected gently, and Ammar closed his eyes.

'It doesn't matter.'

'It does.'

'You don't even know,' Ammar said savagely. 'How much, or even what I've done. You walked away, you were gone for fifteen years—'

'And left you to deal with our father alone.'

He let out a harsh laugh. 'I didn't *deal* with him. I obeyed him. In just about everything.'

'Not everything.'

'You don't know what you're talking about.'

'I did some research, Ammar, in the last few weeks. I know you tried to resist where you could, at least in the last few years.'

'Useless.' Furtive, puny attempts that accomplished so pathetically little, and what about all the years before, years where he'd used and abused his power because it made him feel strong? Years of weakness disguised as strength, immorality hidden under a thin veneer of respectability. It had taken a near-death experience to finally give him the courage and will to change.

'Not useless,' Khalis said, 'to some.'

'To most. And it doesn't change anything. Who I am—'

'No, not who you are. What you did. There's a difference, Ammar, trust me.'

'What do you know about it?' Ammar snarled. He knew he sounded angry and ungrateful, but having this conversation at all was killing him. No, what was killing him was knowing he was losing Noelle. Articulating it to his brother was just the icing on a God-awful cake.

'Actually,' Khalis said mildly, 'I do know something about it. It was Grace who showed me that no one should be defined by their mistakes. Not her, not me, and not even you.'

Ammar fell silent, thinking that through. He knew

Khalis had recently become engaged to this Grace, guessed that their road to true love had had a few bumps. But surely nothing like the mountains and craters he and Noelle were facing. 'What if,' he asked in a low voice, 'there's nothing but mistakes?'

'That's not true.'

'You don't know—'

'Give me a little credit. And stop thinking about who you were or what you did. You told me you'd changed, Ammar, that you wanted to change, and I believed you.' His brother's voice turned wry as he added, 'Admittedly not at first, but I do now. You're a different man, so be different. Show Noelle you've changed.'

I've tried. The words stuck in Ammar's throat. Maybe he hadn't tried enough, or changed enough. Maybe nothing he ever did would be enough.

'Tell her,' Khalis said gently. 'Not just the bad bits, the things you've done in the past. Tell her who you are, what you've endured, and who you want to be. Tell her everything.'

An hour later Ammar pulled up outside Noelle's apartment. He was showered and shaven, even if his eyes were bloodshot and he felt alternately high and drained from both adrenalin and exhaustion.

He got out of the car, murmured a few words to the concierge and headed upstairs. He had just lifted his hand to knock when Noelle opened the door to her apartment. She stilled, staring at him, and it took a few stunned seconds to notice she wasn't dressed for work in one of her dark pencil skirts and crisp white blouses. She wore a pair of capris and a T-shirt and she carried a bag. A suitcase.

She was going somewhere.

'I was going to call you,' she said, not quite looking him in the eye, and Ammar felt his hand fall to his side.

'Were you?'

'Yes…' She hitched her bag higher up on her shoulder. 'It's just everything was such a rush and I need to make my train…'

'Where are you going?'

'Home.' The single word felled him. *Home.* Back to the chateau in Lyon, he knew, and her parents. Not him. He wanted to be her home, her shelter, and yet in that moment he knew he wasn't and she didn't want him to be.

'This is unexpected,' he said, and heard how remote he sounded. How else was he supposed to sound? He'd been about to tell her everything. Perform emotional open-heart surgery on himself for her—no, for *their* sake—and meanwhile she was getting the hell out.

'I know. I'm only going for a few days. It's just I haven't seen them in a while and I think it would be good to…' She trailed off, neither of them bothering to complete her obvious excuse.

Ammar swallowed, stepped back. 'I'll drive you to the train.'

'No—'

'You'd prefer to take a taxi?'

'I just don't want to trouble you,' she muttered, and Ammar felt his heart squeeze. For a moment he couldn't breathe.

'It's no trouble,' he finally said, and turned to head back down the stairs.

They didn't speak in the car. Noelle stared down at her lap, clearly miserable, and Ammar kept his gaze straight ahead. How had it come to this? The better question, he thought savagely, was how could it have not? Could he really be surprised that Noelle wanted out? For that was what this was, he knew. An escape. She'd realised what kind of man he was, what he'd done, just as he'd always feared she would, and now she wanted to leave him. And why shouldn't she?

They reached the Gare de Lyon in silence and Youssef pulled the car in front of the landmark clock tower.

'I'll see you inside,' Ammar said brusquely because, even though he knew it was over, he didn't want to let her go yet.

Noelle didn't answer, but neither did she resist. She muttered her thanks when he picked up her suitcase and strode through the crowd, people parting instinctively for him.

The train had already pulled into the station and they stood on the platform, the air already sultry on a summer's morning. A beautiful day, fresh blue sky and a lemon-yellow sun. And this.

He handed her suitcase to a porter while she fussed with her handbag and tickets, her hair a dark curtain in front of her face. And then there was nothing more to do, nothing more to say but goodbye.

She glanced up at him, her eyes luminous, her mouth trembling. 'Ammar—' she began, her voice so hesitant and sorrowful that he knew he couldn't stand what she was going to say.

He reached for her, sliding his hands along her shoulders and underneath the heavy mass of her gleaming chestnut hair he so loved and pulled her towards him. She came, neither resisting nor accepting, her eyes wide, her jaw slack.

And then he kissed her, hard, with all the pent-up grief and regret and most of all the all-consuming love he felt. He hoped she knew that. He hoped, even now, she knew how much he loved her.

'Goodbye,' he said roughly and, before she could say anything, he turned and was striding away through the crowds, his vision so blurred he could barely see to put one foot in front of the other.

CHAPTER TEN

NOELLE didn't remember much of the train ride to Lyon. She sat and stared out of the window for the two hours it took to travel south, her mind no more than a numb fog. She felt as if she'd just said goodbye to Ammar, a horribly final goodbye, and she hadn't meant to...had she?

She didn't know what she'd meant to do. After last night's revelations she'd wanted only to escape, flee from the tension and heartache and, most of all, herself and her own doubts. She didn't think she could ever travel far enough for that.

The idea of visiting her parents had come with the dawn. The thought of going home, even if just for a weekend, had held a desperate appeal. She could be a child again, just for two days. Life could be simple.

Life, Noelle thought as she stared out of the window of the train, was never simple. And after seeing such terrible, bleak understanding in Ammar's eyes, she couldn't remember just why she had been so desperate to get away.

Her lips still burned from Ammar's kiss. Her body ached. And her heart...her broken heart felt like nothing more than a fistful of jagged splinters, desperate to be stuck back together any which way.

She hadn't thought through her sudden departure. She hadn't thought through anything; she'd endured a sleepless night as her mind replayed the accusations that woman had fired at her. *Ammar Tannous is completely immoral, totally corrupt, and Tannous Enterprises is rotten to the core. If he weren't so damn rich he'd be in jail. So why are you with him?*

That question beat a relentless tattoo in her mind. *Why are you with him? Why are you with him?* And even as her heart insisted the answer was because she loved him, her mind recalled all the things she didn't know. All the things he'd done that even now he wouldn't tell her. She told herself it shouldn't matter, that he was different now, yet she still felt sick with misery. She'd said she loved him, accepted him, and yet she hadn't known what she was accepting. How it would feel.

A tear leaked out of the corner of her eye and she brushed at it impatiently. She knew it was her own fault for getting into this mess, for closing her eyes for so long. She'd *chosen* to be naïve. And now that she wasn't, she no longer knew what to do. How to feel.

Still, it was good to see her father's familiar craggy face at the station. He smiled and hugged her but, as they drove back to their family chateau ten miles outside the city, Noelle thought he seemed distracted.

'Is everything all right?' she asked and her father gave her a quick sideways smile.

'Oh, yes, yes, as ever. But you look so tired, *chérie*. Are you working too hard?'

Noelle managed a smile. 'Maybe a little.' She wasn't ready to tell her parents about Ammar. 'How are things here?' she asked with an attempt at brightness. 'How is Maman?'

Was it her imagination, or did her father's hands tense on the steering wheel? Was she just being paranoid after such a tense confrontation with Ammar?

'Maman is fine,' he said after a pause. 'There is nothing you need to worry about.' Which seemed, Noelle thought, a strange thing to say, considering she had not said she was worried.

'And the bank?' she asked. Her father was an executive at Banque de Lyon, and had been in his position for her entire life.

'You know you need never concern yourself with business matters. If it were up to me, you would not work at all.'

Noelle said nothing. Her father made a similar remark every time she saw him. He might have old-fashioned ideas about men and women's roles, but fortunately he couldn't refuse his only child anything, including a college degree and the opportunity of a career. Even if it was a career she no longer wanted.

What *did* she want?

Noelle gazed blindly out at the placid Rhône, the peaceful pastoral scene of meadows and trees blurring before her eyes. Seeing her father had eased her spirit a little, but she still felt deeply miserable and, worse, guilty. As if she was the one who had done something wrong. And maybe she had.

'Maman will be happy to see you,' her father said and, though he spoke lightly, she heard a tightness in his voice, saw new lines of strain and age from his nose to mouth. Noelle felt a cold pang of fear; she adored her father, had been his spoilt darling for most of her life. She couldn't imagine him not being there, so safe and steady.

Spoilt darling. The throwaway phrase echoed uncomfortably through her. Had it been the actions of a spoilt darling to run back home as soon as things became difficult with Ammar?

Pushing the thought away, she turned to her father again. 'And I can't wait to see her. It's been months.'

An hour later, sitting outside on the terrace with the afternoon sun turning the surface of the Rhône to burnished gold, she felt herself relax. Or at least try to give the appearance of being relaxed, for as Elizabeth Ducasse handed her daughter a glass of iced tea, her eyes narrowed.

'Something has happened.'

Noelle tensed. So much for seeming relaxed. 'What do you mean?'

'Something is wrong.' Elizabeth sat across from her daughter with the English elegance and coolly reserved manner that had attracted Robert Ducasse to her thirty-five years earlier. 'You look terrible, Noelle. Is it a romance? Have you fallen in love again?'

Noelle nearly choked as she sipped her tea. 'If I have, my appearance certainly doesn't recommend it,' she tried to joke, but her voice sounded tight and choked.

Elizabeth pursed her lips. 'I saw a photograph of you in the society pages—with Ammar Tannous.'

Noelle froze, her fingers clenched around her glass. Her mother arched her eyebrows. 'It is him, is it not? It is him again.'

It's always been him. She looked down, saying nothing.

'How has he hurt you this time?' Elizabeth asked, her voice sharpening, and Noelle shook her head.

'He hasn't.' Yet sitting here, with the warmth of the sun and the comfort of her family home, she had a feeling she'd hurt him. Terribly. She'd rejected him as surely as he had her all those years ago. How could she have done such a thing—and so unthinkingly—when she knew how much it hurt? Ammar had frozen her out during their brief marriage, and now she was the one who was wrapping herself in silence, refusing to meet his eye. And running away.

She let out a long shuddering sigh. 'It's complicated,' she said.

Her mother's mouth tightened and she looked away. 'It always is.'

For a moment Noelle wondered if her mother was talking about something else, something bigger. She leaned forward, her troubled thoughts about Ammar momentarily forgotten. 'Maman, is everything all right?'

Her mother swung back sharply to look at her. 'Why do you ask?'

'I don't know,' Noelle said slowly. 'Only that you and Papa both seem a bit tense…' She trailed off because with the sun shining and everything golden and lush all around them, her parents both healthy and well, her vague sense of unease seemed both absurd and paranoid. The tension of the last few weeks with Ammar must be really taking their toll.

'We're fine,' Elizabeth said firmly, but she didn't meet Noelle's gaze as she said it and Noelle wondered what, if anything, her parents were hiding.

She found out the next day. She'd spent another restless night barely able to sleep, her mind going over every poignant memory of the last few weeks, even as her body cried out for Ammar. She missed sleeping in the solid strength of his embrace, of being woken up by his playful, nudging kisses. She missed the startled suddenness of his smile, as if he were surprising both of them with his own happiness. She missed his wry jokes, so carefully made, as if he really had to think about it, and the way his gaze seemed to burn when he looked at her.

She missed *him*. More than she'd ever thought possible, even more than she'd missed him when she'd stumbled out of the hotel in Rome that awful night and gone—

Here. She'd run back home, just as she'd done now. Instead of facing him, *them*, whatever was causing the problem, she'd run away. The realisation made Noelle flinch with regret and shame.

And yet the safety and security of the home she'd always known crumbled to dust when she came downstairs to find her parents facing each other across the dining room table, a newspaper spread out on it.

'How could you?' Elizabeth's voice rang out coldly and Robert glanced at Noelle, his mouth tightening.

'Let's not talk like this, Elizabeth. In front of—'

'It's in front of the whole world.' Elizabeth gestured to the newspaper. 'If you had to have an affair, could you not have chosen someone more discreet?'

Robert's mouth tightened. 'And is that all you care about? What's presented in the papers?'

'Would you prefer I be heartbroken?' Elizabeth asked sharply, but her words ended on a choked sob and she turned away, one fist pressed to her mouth.

Sighing tiredly, Robert shot Noelle an apologetic glance before leaving the room.

Numbly, Noelle stepped forward. 'Maman, what on earth is going on?'

Elizabeth simply gestured to the newspaper. 'It appears you've come at a bad time.'

With a hard-beating heart Noelle picked up the paper and read the three-inch headline in disbelief. *Family Man's Mistress Tells All.*

She sank down in one of the dining room chairs as she read the article, each word dousing her in disbelief. The article was an interview with her father's mistress. A woman he'd been seeing for nearly twenty years.

I can't live a lie any more, the woman was claimed to have said. *I need to tell the truth about Robert and me. He's loved me for so long.*

Eventually she looked up from the newspaper. 'Did you…did you know?'

Elizabeth didn't answer for a long moment. She stood in front of the window, her back to Noelle, the sunlight creating a halo of gold around her bowed head. 'I suspected,' she said quietly.

'All this time—'

'I didn't know how long. But something, yes. I suspected something.'

'Oh, Maman.' Noelle felt her chest tighten, her throat squeezed. She could barely get the words out. 'How could you…how could you stay, knowing—'

'Oh, Noelle, you can be such a child sometimes.'

The accusation stung. 'Am I a child for thinking you should have more from your marriage—'

'No—' her mother cut her off '—you're a child if you believe it makes a difference when you love someone.' She turned to face her daughter, her expression one of both stubbornness and sorrow. 'I loved him. I've always loved him, and so I just didn't think of anything else. Anything that would come between us.'

Noelle shook her head slowly even as realisation stole through her with cold, creeping fingers. Hadn't she been just like her mother, sinking her head into the sand, refusing to think of anything that might disturb her untarnished view of the world, of Ammar?

'I'm sorry,' Elizabeth said after a moment. 'This is more of a shock to you than me, I think.'

'What…what happens now?'

'I don't know. Now that this woman has told the papers…they'll have a field day. Robert always liked to be thought of as a family man.' Her mouth twisted bitterly.

'A field day,' Noelle said slowly. 'You mean, more press?'

'I imagine,' Elizabeth said grimly, 'they're gathering outside right now, the vultures. This will be a big story, Noelle. Your father is a prominent man. Tabloids sell scandal.' She sighed. 'It might be better if we go away for a while. To the Caribbean, perhaps. We could have some time together. Would you like that?'

Noelle stared at her mother in disbelief. She could not believe what she was suggesting, as if a holiday would make things better. As if she could even think of a holiday when her family was falling apart. Yet perhaps that was the only way Elizabeth had been able to live with her husband's faithlessness: by closing her eyes. Smiling and pretending it didn't matter, it didn't exist. Just like she had done with Ammar's own difficult history. But she wasn't going to run away this time. She needed to face both her father and Ammar. 'No,' she said quietly. 'I don't think so, Maman. I'm going to stay here.'

'As you wish.'

The same words Ammar had used last night. *As you wish.* But she didn't wish for any of this. And wishing didn't do any good. It was time for action, for truth. 'I'm going to talk to Papa,' she said, and rose from her chair.

She found him in his study, going over some papers as if it were a normal day, as if nothing had happened. Noelle leaned against the door, the pain and shock of it all streaking through her again.

'Aren't you,' she asked, 'going to say anything?'

He looked up, guarded, guilty, like a little boy who had been caught stealing sweets. 'I'm sorry, Noelle. I never meant to hurt you.'

The words were rote. She could not tell if he meant them. 'Why?' she asked, the one word scraping her throat. 'Why, all this time, for so long?'

Robert looked down. 'I was lonely,' he said quietly. 'I

travelled for work, you know that, and your mother was busy with you, with her charities—' He sighed, shrugged. 'I never meant to hurt anyone.' He looked up at her, spreading his hands as if she would now absolve him. Excuses. He had given her nothing but excuses.

Noelle felt everything inside her clench in a hard fist of understanding. Ammar had never spoken like this. He'd been honest, so excruciatingly honest with her about his faults. He had never lied or dissembled. He hadn't even offered one excuse. He had, in fact, told her the worst of himself, how he'd once enjoyed wielding that kind of power, wanting her to know everything. Hoping she would still love him. And she'd turned away. She'd rejected him, as surely as he had her all those years ago.

Noelle closed her eyes, her treatment of Ammar as well as the fresh betrayal of her father making her whole body throb with the pain of it all.

'Noelle,' her father said, 'I am sorry.'

She opened her eyes. 'Will you stop seeing this woman? Will you go to counselling with Maman? Will you *change*?'

Her father recoiled slightly, saying nothing. And that, Noelle knew, was his answer.

Ammar had changed. Ammar had *wanted* to change, and every choice he'd made had been a way to live differently. To be the man he wanted to be.

With her by his side.

That was where she wanted to be, right now, for ever. Yet would he take her back? Could he accept and forgive her when she'd shown him how much she doubted him?

The day passed in a haze of misery and the next morning Noelle woke to a swarm of paparazzi outside the chateau. Her parents were both at the breakfast table, stony-faced and silent.

'I'm going to leave,' Noelle said quietly. She couldn't

bear the awful tension that had sprung up not just between her parents, but between them all. Every relationship felt tainted now, irrevocably altered, even if her mother wanted to pretend otherwise.

Elizabeth glanced up from her tea. 'Wait a day at least. The reporters will be crawling all over you.' She made a little moue of distaste, as if this was unpleasant but bearable. Noelle felt like shaking her.

'I don't care about the reporters.' She glanced at her father. 'Are you both just going to go on, pretending nothing has happened? What about this other woman, Papa?'

'Don't talk like that, Noelle,' Elizabeth said sharply, and her father just looked down. He was letting her mother cover for him. Her father, she realised bleakly, was a weak man. A kind, loving and horribly weak man.

Not like Ammar. How much strength had it taken to decide to change Tannous Enterprises for the better? To face all his foes—as well as his allies—and state he was going to be different?

Because he *was* different.

She knew that now, knew that no matter what he had done in his past, no matter what he'd *wanted* to do, he was different now. Strong and wise and good.

The man she loved.

'Goodbye,' she said, her throat aching, and turned towards the door.

The reporters were waiting for her, with their cameras and questions, the flashes and the noise. Noelle blinked and stiffened, every word an assault.

Did you know about your father's affair? Will your mother divorce him? Do you feel betrayed?

Invasive, awful questions. Noelle tried to ignore them as she shouldered through the reporters, but the cameras went off in her face and for a moment she couldn't see.

She stumbled on the stone steps in front of the chateau and not one person moved to help her. Someone took a photo.

She wished, deeply and painfully, for Ammar to be there. To feel his arms around her, to know she was safe. For she knew that now, had always known it. She was safe, utterly, wonderfully safe with Ammar. Safe and loved.

Tears rose in her throat and crowded her eyes but she blinked them back fiercely. No more tears. Now was the time for action. She would find Ammar, she would tell him how sorry she was—the thought was both daunting and necessary.

She straightened, started making her way through the crowd again. She tried to blank out the barrage of baiting questions when she heard another voice, stronger, deeper.

'Noelle.'

She looked up and her gaze arrowed straight in on the tall, imposing figure shouldering his way through the reporters. It was Ammar.

CHAPTER ELEVEN

THE world fell away, the reporters and their questions completely unimportant as Ammar came towards her. Noelle didn't think she'd ever been so glad to see someone. See *him*. He had a day's worth of stubble on his strong jaw, shadows under his eyes. He looked tired, anxious and utterly wonderful.

'Ammar—' she whispered, and he reached for her hand.

'I'm taking you away from here.' The reporters had fallen back for a moment, stunned by the drama playing itself out right before their eyes, but when Ammar took her hand they started again.

'*Mademoiselle*, are you seeing Tannous? Do you know the things he's done?'

'Do you approve of your father's actions? What about Tannous?'

'Ignore them,' Ammar said roughly, but she knew from the way his hand tensed over hers that he couldn't ignore them. Not enough.

Ammar pushed through the reporters, still holding her hand, and led her to the car he'd parked by the chateau's gates. He helped her in before getting in on the driver's side and soon they were speeding away, the reporters far behind still desperate to take a few last snaps.

Neither of them spoke, and when Noelle sneaked a

glance at Ammar she saw how tense he looked, even angry. His jaw was bunched tight, his eyes narrowed as he navigated the road towards Lyon.

'Thank you,' she finally managed, her voice shaky, and Ammar just nodded tersely. She had no idea what he was thinking, or even why he had come. 'Where's Youssef?' she asked instead of the far more important questions shrieking inside her.

'Back in Paris. I wanted to come alone.'

'How…how did you know?'

Ammar lifted one powerful shoulder in a half-shrug. 'It's in all the newspapers.'

'Of course it is,' Noelle murmured. She stared blindly out of the window; Ammar had turned onto the Route Nationale Seven towards Paris. 'I'm glad you did come,' she said after a moment, awkwardly. 'I…I don't think I've ever been so glad to see someone.'

'I'm glad I could be there.' Noelle couldn't tell a thing from his tone. 'I know you loved him very much.'

'I still love him,' Noelle said quietly, and she knew it to be true, despite all the disappointment and heartache. 'Did you think I wouldn't?'

Ammar flexed his fingers on the steering wheel. 'I know what it's like to learn the truth about your father.'

She glanced at him, saw he was staring straight ahead. 'Is that what happened to you?'

'Yes.'

'Tell me.'

Ammar said nothing for a long moment. The small space of the car felt intimate, the silence hushed and expectant. Noelle felt her heart beating hard. 'I was eight,' he finally said quietly. 'Up until then, I had what I think was a normal childhood, playing with my brother, spoiling my little sister.' Noelle had not even known he had siblings.

'Then, on my eighth birthday, my father decided to take an interest in me. He'd been a distant figure before, coming back to the island to visit us, give us some ridiculously lavish gifts and then disappear again. I adored him from afar, and so did my brother Khalis.' He paused, rolling his shoulders as if to rid them of the tension that kept them so painfully rigid. 'When I turned eight my father called me into his office. I suppose I thought he might give me a present. I remember feeling excited, happy.' Noelle felt tears rise even though she didn't know what was coming next. She didn't want to know. Listening was painful, yet she knew this memory was the beginning and perhaps even the key to understanding Ammar.

'He hit me,' Ammar said quietly. He sounded sad rather than angry. 'Hard, across the face, with no warning. I fell to the floor, my head reeling, my mouth bleeding. I couldn't believe what had happened.'

'Why?' Noelle whispered. From what Ammar had already told her about Balkri Tannous, she knew she shouldn't be surprised and yet she was. Surprised and horrified.

'My first lesson,' Ammar explained with a grim smile. 'Never trust anyone, not even those you love. Always be on your guard. He stood over me and told me that while I lay on the floor and tried not to cry.'

'Oh, Ammar.' Instinctively she reached over and placed her hand on his leg, needing to touch him.

Ammar let out a resigned and weary sigh. 'I told you that so you'd know I understand what it's like to have your hero thrown off his pedestal. In that moment the pain of knowing what he was like was worse than any blow he could have dealt me.'

'Yes,' she whispered. 'I can see that.'

'But I didn't tell you so you'd feel sorry for me,' he continued, his voice becoming hard. 'I don't want your pity, Noelle. I've never wanted it.'

'I don't pity you.'

'And I'm tired of pointing to my past as the reason I am who I am now.' He shook his head, his face so bleak Noelle felt her nearly-whole heart start to splinter again. 'God, I am so tired of it.'

'Then maybe,' Noelle whispered, 'we should think about the future instead.' Ammar glanced at her sharply, and she gave him a tremulous smile. There was so much more she wanted to say, yet everything felt as if it had lodged in a huge, hot lump in her chest and she wasn't sure if she could get anything out.

Neither of them spoke for a moment, and when Ammar finally broke the taut silence it was in a carefully bland voice. 'Do you want me to take you back to your apartment?'

The thought brought only dread. 'How far are we from Paris?'

'About an hour.'

'Do you think the press will have discovered where I live?'

'Undoubtedly.'

Noelle let out a groan. 'I can't bear the thought of fighting through more crowds, or having them snap my picture.' Or listening to their awful, slyly mocking questions.

'We don't have to return to Paris,' Ammar said quietly, and Noelle felt a thrill of expectation ripple through her.

'Where would we go?'

'There's a place near here. A few more minutes.'

'A place?'

'Just a place I know.' He stared straight ahead, not looking at her. Curiosity added to her adrenalin-rush of anticipation.

'All right,' she said, and Ammar glanced at her, his expression an unguarded mix of wariness and hope.

'All right?'

'Take me there.' And really she didn't care where he took her. She'd go anywhere with him.

They drove in silence down the motorway, and after a little while Ammar turned off onto a narrow country lane. Noelle gazed out of the window as they drove through several sleepy villages, their deserted squares indolent under a noontime sun. Then he turned down an even narrower lane, with just one house at its end. Noelle sat up straighter, her curiosity truly piqued.

Ammar pulled in front of the house and killed the engine. Noelle gazed in bemusement at the rambling house, a riot of flowers climbing over its yellow stone walls. 'What is this place?'

'Come and see.'

Still curious, she got out of the car. The house was utterly charming, with the wrought iron railings in front of each shuttered window, the happy clutter of terracotta pots filled with geraniums by the long, smooth stone that served as a front step. She loved it all, but she still didn't know where she was. Was Ammar taking her to *visit* someone?

He slid a key out of his pocket and opened the front door. Holding her breath, Noelle stepped inside. The house was comfortably furnished, with scattered sofas arranged around an inglenook fireplace and a pair of French windows leading out to a terraced garden. Sunshine spilled into the room, bathing everything in gold. Noelle turned around slowly in a circle, taking it all in, then turned to Ammar.

'Where are we?'

He stood by the door, the key still in his hand, a funny,

sad sort of smile on his face. 'Don't you recognise this place?'

'I've never been here before.'

'I know.'

'But—' She stopped suddenly, realisation dawning... the way the sun crept over the horizon, slowly, spreading its healing light. 'It's our house,' she said slowly, 'isn't it? Our little house outside Paris.'

Ammar nodded and she shook her head, still hardly able to believe it. 'I didn't even think you remembered.'

'Oh, I remembered.' And she knew from the throb in his voice that he'd held hard to their dream. 'In any case, I bought this house years ago.'

'You *bought* it? When?' But of course she already knew. Ten years ago, when they were to be married.

'It was your wedding present,' Ammar said quietly, and Noelle let out a choked cry. He was so wonderfully thoughtful, so achingly tender, and yet she couldn't bear it. She felt the weight of her own guilt like a stone inside her, bearing her down.

'Noelle—' He took a step towards her, his eyes shadowed. 'We don't...you don't have to like it, or live here. I didn't bring you here for that. I just wanted to show you... how much...'

She shook her head, flung out one hand. 'Don't.'

He stopped, his whole body tense. 'What?'

'I need to say something first.'

He looked so guarded, so uncertain, and that was her fault. 'What do you want to say?'

'That I'm sorry,' she said quietly. 'For leaving the way I did. I didn't... I didn't want it to be like that.'

Ammar still looked wary. 'It is a small matter,' he said, and her heart twisted inside her. She'd wanted him to help her, to acknowledge what had happened back in Paris, and yet from the veiled look in his eyes and the tension in his body she knew he wasn't going to—and she understood why. He was guarding his heart, just as she had been. She'd hurt him, just as he'd hurt her all those years ago. No wonder he was wary. How could she *not* understand that?

'It isn't a small matter,' she said quietly. 'It's a big one, at least to me, and I think it is to you as well. I admit, I started feeling scared when we were in Paris—'

Ammar had angled his head away from her so he was gazing out of the window, his body still tense. 'Of me?' he asked, and she shook her head.

'No—I've never been afraid of you. *Never.* It's just… I felt there were all these things I didn't know, and they kept me from feeling close to you. And when a woman approached me at the ball—'

'I don't want to hear it,' Ammar cut across her, his hands clenching into fists.

'I won't tell you,' Noelle said, her heart hammering so hard now, hard enough to hurt, 'because it doesn't matter. I admit, I was startled. I hadn't let myself think of it. Think of the past, and the things you've done. I'd just glossed over it in my mind.'

'I know,' he said, his voice so low she had to strain to hear him. 'I didn't want you to think of it.'

'And it shook me, all this doubt I was feeling. It made me wonder—' She stopped suddenly, not wanting to finish that thought. To admit how weak she'd been.

'If you loved me,' Ammar filled in, and she blinked hard.

'I just didn't know how it would *feel*,' she whispered. 'To know those things. And it made all the old memories and fears came back. I wondered if I really knew you at all. It was my problem, Ammar.'

'I see,' he said, and he sounded so remote that Noelle took a step towards him.

'I'm sorry for doubting you,' she whispered. 'And doubting what I felt for you. I should have stayed, I should have told you all this, I know. I should have been honest, and maybe that would have helped. But I was afraid of being honest, of risking what we had because it felt so fragile—'

'I know how that feels,' Ammar said quietly, and she felt some of the awful tension leave her body. 'I should have told you the whole truth a long time ago. The night of our wedding—it wasn't just because of the memories that I stayed away. My father spoke to me.'

'He woke you up, didn't he,' Noelle said, understanding now. Understanding so much. 'From our dream world.'

He nodded. 'When he spoke to me, I realised how deluded I'd been, thinking we could have something, that things could change.' He paused, swallowed. 'That you could love me.'

'Oh, Ammar.'

'I convinced myself I was protecting you by leaving, and maybe I was, but I was also protecting myself. I would have rather walked away than have you know the truth about me.'

'But I know the truth now.'

'I know you do.'

'And I love you.'

He jerked his gaze back to her, clearly startled.

'I love you,' Noelle said again. 'And I'm sorry, so sorry for hurting you and for leaving you the way I did. I wasn't thinking properly. I just wanted some space to get away— not from you, even, but from myself and my own desperate thoughts.' She took another step towards him. 'The moment I got on that train I felt I'd made a mistake. And when I arrived in Lyon I felt even worse. I thought I was going home, but I wasn't. I left my home when I left you.'

Noelle saw a blaze of feeling in his eyes. 'Do you mean that?'

'*Yes.* It took me leaving to realise how much I wanted to stay. How little any of the gossip or rumours—'

'It's not just gossip or rumours, Noelle. You know that.' He sounded so bleak that her heart ached for him.

'Yes, I know that. I realise you did things on your father's command—'

'Don't let my father take all the blame. I was a grown man. I didn't like everything I did, but I enjoyed the power. I liked feeling in control.'

'After the kind of childhood you had, I can under-stand—'

'Don't,' he said harshly. 'Don't explain it away. It was wrong.'

She swallowed. 'I know that.'

'I could have made other choices. My brother did. Khalis. He left when he was twenty-one, turned his back on my father and started his own company. He was strong enough to leave—'

'Sometimes,' Noelle whispered, 'it's stronger to stay.'

For a moment his face crumpled, almost as if he would cry, and then he shook his head. 'No. Never.'

'Yes,' she said firmly. 'It is. And I know I can't even imagine what you endured, Ammar. I'm not excusing you, or any of the things you did. I know you did things that were wrong, or even criminal. I know and I accept it, be-cause I know you've changed. I know what kind of man you want to be, what kind of man you *are.* And I'm ab-solving you, because you can't carry that crippling weight around any more.'

He stared at her hungrily, as if she were offering something he didn't dare believe in. 'You have no idea,' he began, 'even now, what I've—'

'I don't *need* to know,' she said, walking towards him, full of a wonderful, singing certainty now. 'I know you, and I love you. I see what you're doing with the company now, and I see how tender you are with me, and I believe in you utterly. I trust you, Ammar, with my life. With my heart.' She stood before him, her whole body trembling, a tremulous smile on her lips. 'I love you. So very much.'

Ammar stared at her for a long, fathomless moment. If only she knew what he was thinking. If only she knew that he believed her, *trusted* her—

Then his face crumpled and he looked away, blinking hard. Noelle's breath caught in her chest. 'Oh, Ammar.' Without needing to think about what she was doing, she crossed to him and drew him into her arms. She felt his whole body shudder with the force of his feeling. Had he ever grieved for the boy he'd been, full of hope and happiness, waiting for his father's birthday present? Had he grieved for the man he'd become, harsh, unyielding, loveless, even cruel?

Only with the acknowledgement of that grief could he believe in the man she already knew he was, knew with her entire being. Her whole heart.

After a long moment he lifted his head, looked at her with damp eyes. She gazed back, full of certainty, buoyant with it. And then Ammar pulled her to him and, as his lips found hers, she wrapped her arms around him, stood on tiptoe and pulled him as close as he could get.

He kissed her deeply, his mouth moving on hers, seeking and finding. Pleasure and relief, joy and desire coursed through her as she returned the kiss with all the passion and love she felt.

Finally, with a shuddering breath he released her, rested

his forehead against hers. 'I love you,' he said softly. 'So much. And I'm sorry, so very sorry, for ever hurting you.'

In answer, in absolution, she kissed him again, softly. The past was truly finished now. They had only to look towards the future. Their future.

With a playful smile she looped her arms around his neck. 'Does this place have a bedroom?'

His mouth quirked upwards. 'Three.'

'And does one have a big bed and a fireplace?' She'd been very specific about their dream house.

'And a chestnut tree outside.'

She laughed, the sound of pure joy, because she couldn't believe he'd remembered everything, he'd thought of everything. He'd made every one of her dreams a reality.

'Then let's go upstairs and find it,' she said and, smiling, her hand in his, Ammar turned and showed her the way.

EPILOGUE

Three months later

NOELLE lay on the bed, her whole body tingling with anticipation. Tonight was her wedding night.

It had been a beautiful, wonderful day. They had had a quiet ceremony at a small church in Lyon, just a handful of family and friends attending. That was how they both wanted it; they'd had the big wedding before. Today was something different.

It had been good to have people there, the people who mattered. Her parents had come, presenting a united front for her sake although their marriage was still in jeopardy. Her father had, at least, stopped seeing his mistress. Her mother still looked strained, but hopeful. Who knew what would happen? Noelle hoped her parents could find even a fraction of the happiness she felt now.

Ammar's brother Khalis and his new wife Grace had also come, smiling, so obviously in love. As in love as Noelle was with Ammar. Her husband.

She shivered, the night air cool on her bare skin. No virginal white peignoir for her tonight. She wore nothing at all. She smiled as she thought of Ammar seeing her as he came into the suite they were staying in for this first night of their marriage, an opulent set of rooms in the Château de Bagnols, once an ancient fortress and now a world-class hotel. A fire flickered in the grate and shadows danced across the huge four-poster bed. He'd let her come upstairs first, knowing she wanted to get ready. Knowing, just as Noelle did, that it needed to happen this way.

She smiled and stretched, impatience warring with her excitement. Surely Ammar would arrive soon. She felt no fear or worry, only a glorious anticipation for what was to come.

Tonight, and many more nights. The rest of their lives.

She heard footsteps, and the doorknob turned. The door opened and smiling, his eyes alight with love, Ammar came into the room.

* * * * *

Mills & Boon® Hardback

September 2012

ROMANCE

Unlocking her Innocence	Lynne Graham
Santiago's Command	Kim Lawrence
His Reputation Precedes Him	Carole Mortimer
The Price of Retribution	Sara Craven
Just One Last Night	Helen Brooks
The Greek's Acquisition	Chantelle Shaw
The Husband She Never Knew	Kate Hewitt
When Only Diamonds Will Do	Lindsay Armstrong
The Couple Behind the Headlines	Lucy King
The Best Mistake of Her Life	Aimee Carson
The Valtieri Baby	Caroline Anderson
Slow Dance with the Sheriff	Nikki Logan
Bella's Impossible Boss	Michelle Douglas
The Tycoon's Secret Daughter	Susan Meier
She's So Over Him	Joss Wood
Return of the Last McKenna	Shirley Jump
Once a Playboy…	Kate Hardy
Challenging the Nurse's Rules	Janice Lynn

MEDICAL

Her Motherhood Wish	Anne Fraser
A Bond Between Strangers	Scarlet Wilson
The Sheikh and the Surrogate Mum	Meredith Webber
Tamed by her Brooding Boss	Joanna Neil

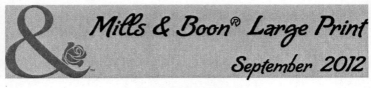

Mills & Boon® Large Print
September 2012

ROMANCE

A Vow of Obligation	Lynne Graham
Defying Drakon	Carole Mortimer
Playing the Greek's Game	Sharon Kendrick
One Night in Paradise	Maisey Yates
Valtieri's Bride	Caroline Anderson
The Nanny Who Kissed Her Boss	Barbara McMahon
Falling for Mr Mysterious	Barbara Hannay
The Last Woman He'd Ever Date	Liz Fielding
His Majesty's Mistake	Jane Porter
Duty and the Beast	Trish Morey
The Darkest of Secrets	Kate Hewitt

HISTORICAL

Lady Priscilla's Shameful Secret	Christine Merrill
Rake with a Frozen Heart	Marguerite Kaye
Miss Cameron's Fall from Grace	Helen Dickson
Society's Most Scandalous Rake	Isabelle Goddard
The Taming of the Rogue	Amanda McCabe

MEDICAL

Falling for the Sheikh She Shouldn't	Fiona McArthur
Dr Cinderella's Midnight Fling	Kate Hardy
Brought Together by Baby	Margaret McDonagh
One Month to Become a Mum	Louisa George
Sydney Harbour Hospital: Luca's Bad Girl	Amy Andrews
The Firebrand Who Unlocked His Heart	Anne Fraser

Mills & Boon® Hardback

October 2012

ROMANCE

Banished to the Harem	Carol Marinelli
Not Just the Greek's Wife	Lucy Monroe
A Delicious Deception	Elizabeth Power
Painted the Other Woman	Julia James
A Game of Vows	Maisey Yates
A Devil in Disguise	Caitlin Crews
Revelations of the Night Before	Lynn Raye Harris
Defying her Desert Duty	Annie West
The Wedding Must Go On	Robyn Grady
The Devil and the Deep	Amy Andrews
Taming the Brooding Cattleman	Marion Lennox
The Rancher's Unexpected Family	Myrna Mackenzie
Single Dad's Holiday Wedding	Patricia Thayer
Nanny for the Millionaire's Twins	Susan Meier
Truth-Or-Date.com	Nina Harrington
Wedding Date with Mr Wrong	Nicola Marsh
The Family Who Made Him Whole	Jennifer Taylor
The Doctor Meets Her Match	Annie Claydon

MEDICAL

A Socialite's Christmas Wish	Lucy Clark
Redeeming Dr Riccardi	Leah Martyn
The Doctor's Lost-and-Found Heart	Dianne Drake
The Man Who Wouldn't Marry	Tina Beckett

ROMANCE

A Secret Disgrace	Penny Jordan
The Dark Side of Desire	Julia James
The Forbidden Ferrara	Sarah Morgan
The Truth Behind his Touch	Cathy Williams
Plain Jane in the Spotlight	Lucy Gordon
Battle for the Soldier's Heart	Cara Colter
The Navy SEAL's Bride	Soraya Lane
My Greek Island Fling	Nina Harrington
Enemies at the Altar	Melanie Milburne
In the Italian's Sights	Helen Brooks
In Defiance of Duty	Caitlin Crews

HISTORICAL

The Duchess Hunt	Elizabeth Beacon
Marriage of Mercy	Carla Kelly
Unbuttoning Miss Hardwick	Deb Marlowe
Chained to the Barbarian	Carol Townend
My Fair Concubine	Jeannie Lin

MEDICAL

Georgie's Big Greek Wedding?	Emily Forbes
The Nurse's Not-So-Secret Scandal	Wendy S. Marcus
Dr Right All Along	Joanna Neil
Summer With A French Surgeon	Margaret Barker
Sydney Harbour Hospital: Tom's Redemption	Fiona Lowe
Doctor on Her Doorstep	Annie Claydon

0912 GEN STD LP